CHECKING OUT

In front of them stood a tall, slender European with a Soviet Makarov pistol in his left fist. He motioned with the muzzle, a menace and an order.

"Come out," he curtly told them.

The Russian agent apparently did not see the thick-barreled High Standard in the Penetrator's hand. Mark brought it up and shot Mikiael Koretsa low in the abdomen. His last two rounds had been standard solid-point bullets, with no poison. Koretsa staggered backward and started to fire the Makarov. Mark shot him a second time, in the left kneecap.

Comrade Koretsa went down with a moan that grew into a high-pitched, nearly silent whine of agony. Samantha kicked his pistol away and they met over the body.

"Into the elevator with him," the Penetrator decided. "We haven't much time. We go down two floors to your room, stash the bodies and question this one. Then we have to get out of this hotel."

Sam nodded grimly. "Somehow the thought of staying here has lost a lot of its appeal."

THE PENETRATOR SERIES:

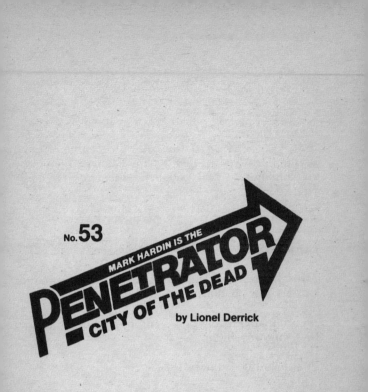

No. **53**

MARK HARDIN IS THE

PENETRATOR

CITY OF THE DEAD

by Lionel Derrick

PINNACLE BOOKS **NEW YORK**

PENETRATOR #53: CITY OF THE DEAD

An original Pinnacle Books edition, published for the first time anywhere.

First printing, January 1984

Special Acknowledgement: Mark Roberts

ISBN: 0-523-41958-9

Can. ISBN: 0-523-43092-2

Cover illustration by George Wilson

Printed in the United States of America

PINNACLE BOOKS, INC.
1430 Broadway
New York, New York 10018

9 8 7 6 5 4 3 2 1

DEDICATION

This book is humbly dedicated to all those who courageously fight Soviet aggression in Afghanistan and to the memory of all those who have been murdered by the Soviet use of Yellow Rain, "Blue-X" and "The Flash" in Southeast Asia and Afghanistan. May their sacrifice not be in vain. . . . Let the world be the judge.

L.D.

CITY
OF THE
DEAD

1

HAPPY HONEYMOON

Deeply inset entranceways created pools of black shadow from the soft park lights of the condominium complex in Salt Lake City. The form of a tall, broad-shouldered man blended into one of them as though only another ebony shade. His hands went to the door and soon undid the dead-bolt lock and standard, in-the-knob cylinder latch. He eased the portal open and slipped inside.

The intruder carefully worked his way around articles of furniture and approached the stairway to the second floor. There he paused, listening, then snapped on the lights. Quickly he climbed, taking the steps two at a time. In the upper hall he turned to the left, toward the master bedroom, and grasped the knob of the closed door. With a twist he released the latch and flung the partition wide. A touch of the switch and light flooded the room.

"Angie, wake up. It's me, Mark. Wake up, hon."

"W-wha ... What is it?" a sleepy voice replied.

"Wake up, Angie," Mark Hardin repeated. "Get dressed. I'll start the kids on it. Pack a few things and let's go."

Fully awake now, Angie Dillon gazed wide-eyed at the big, smiling man who stood in the doorway. Her thoughts raced, blurred with speed until she hit on one possible course. Sudden fear tinged her words. "Is it . . . ? Is something wrong? Are we in danger?"

"No, no danger," Mark returned through a laugh. "I'm taking you to where there will never be any threat again."

"Where is that?"

"You're all going to the Stronghold. From there we're going to San Diego to get married and then on a long honeymoon. A two-year honeymoon on a beautiful blue-water boat that will take us and the twins around the world."

"Mark, Mark, have you lost your mind? I . . . I thought you said marriage was out of the question. T-the, ah, Penetrator thing and all. It would be too dangerous to us."

"The Penetrator is going to cease to exist. We take two years traveling around the world, educating the kids and having fun. Then . . . well, we'll see. But your home, from now on will be in Willard Haskins' underground fortress. Nothing and no one can hurt you or Karen or Kevin there. You . . ." Mark paused, suddenly as uncertain as any young suitor. "You do love me, don't you? And you do want to be married, don't you?"

One of Angie's firm, competent hands went to her mouth to stifle a giggle. She tossed her

long auburn tresses and delighted mirth sparkled in her green eyes. "This is the wildest,
most insane proposal I have ever had. Most
likely that any girl has experienced. But . . ."
She waited, enjoying the uncertainty of this
ever-composed, always positive man. "Yes,
darling. I do love you and want to be your
wife."

She slid from the bed, entirely nude, her
evenly tanned body a golden glow in the bright
lights. Mark stared at her slim, curvaceous
figure with longing and appreciation, based
on intimate knowledge that spanned the years.
Then he turned away and went to Kevin's
room.

Tousled blond hair lay on a crisp pastel-
blue pillow slip, above a tanned, freckle-dusted
face that looked much younger than its thirteen years. When Mark turned on the light, a
small, bronzed arm came up to shade closed
eyes, revealing a smooth, bare shoulder. The
tall figure with jet hair and snapping black
eyes stepped closer to the bed.

"Time to get up, Kevin. This is Mark. Open
your eyes."

Kevin Dillon blinked, stirred and sat upright,
the bedclothes spilling off him. "W-what is it,
Mark? What time?"

"Time to get up, get dressed and get packed.
We're all going on a long trip."

"Alll riiight!" the boy enthused, always ready
for an adventure with this best of all friends.
"Where're we going?'

"That will take some explaining. For now,

get your clothes on, pack what you'll need for two or three days and wait downstairs."

Mark turned away and went toward Kevin's twin sister's bedroom. Behind him, the naked boy leaped out of bed and began crawling into undershorts, Hang Ten sport shorts and a pullover knit shirt. Mark entered Karen's pink-and-white chintz-and-lace room, lit the light and bent over her sleeping form. He kissed her lightly on the cheek. Her eyes popped open and she sat up,

"Mark! You're finally going to marry Mom, right?" she announced with an assurance that seemed almost preternatural. Except for the budding breasts on her unclothed chest, she looked a carbon copy of Kevin.

"You amaze me, sweetheart. That's exactly what it's about." He repeated the packing instructions and returned to Angie's room to watch her brush her luxurious auburn locks.

"Yumm, you look good enough to eat."

"Not now," Angie teased. "Wait until the honeymoon."

"Once I have you in my power, far out to sea, I intend to do a great deal more than *that*," Mark offered in a lecherous tone. "Now hurry. The kids are already packing."

"What do I take?"

"The bare essentials for now. Uh, well, less bare than this family is accustomed to run around. Willard Haskins would be scandalized."

"Who is he?"

"I'll explain it all on the flight to the Stronghold. The Mooney is out at the airport, fueled and ready. Let's go," he concluded with all the impatience of an eloping bravo of Renaissance Italy.

In the living room, ten minutes later, he offered more explanation. "I've arranged for a moving company to come in and load everything up. It will be delivered to San Diego. There you can all pick what you need for the trip."

"Why San Diego?" Angie inquired.

"You are going to flat disappear. No trace, nothing. After we return, we'll all live at the Stronghold. By then, all your stuff will be moved in and this place sold."

"What trip?" Kevin and Karen asked together.

"A two-year cruise around the world." The youngsters jumped up and down and cheered. Small in stature, they appeared to be at least three years younger than their age. "I've bought a boat, a thirty-eight-foot motor sailer, and your mom can teach you during that time. No skipping school. Afterward, Willard, ah, Professor Haskins can continue your education as well."

"Boo!" the twins chorussed, making thumbs-down gestures.

"Hey! The whole voyage is going to be a learning experience. And knowledge is too damned important for anyone to pass up a chance at more education whenever and wherever they can get it."

That mollified the twins, but Angie turned a worried expression on Mark. "Why now? So all of a sudden like?"

Mark sighed, his high, bronze forehead creased with lines of deep concern. ''Because . . . everything seems to be closing in. I've been forced to take bigger and bigger chances. The odds are running out. At times I think I am becoming a danger to myself. If so, I am also a tremendous danger to those who know me. At the Stronghold you will be protected, anonymous. No one can get to you. And you are all too . . . too precious to me to see anything happen. Aw . . . hell, I'm no good at this sort of thing. Kids, load up my car. It's parked in the first slot at the end of the walk. Angie, put the keys in this envelope and we'll mail it to the movers on the way to the airport. Next stop, California.''

On the two-hour flight to the landing strip in the Mojave Desert outside Barstow, California, the man known to the world only as the Penetrator explained how he had purchased the boat, which he had renamed *Bona Fortuna*, and the itinerary of their two-year cruise. For the first time in all the long, tumultuous years, Mark Hardin felt completely relaxed. He had made the right decision, surely and positively, as he had made another so long ago.

Mark Hardin, the Penetrator, had not always been a man who distrusted every shadow, who lived on the edge of instant death at the hands of criminals or police. He had been a combat veteran of Vietnam, later of the seamy silent war of army counterintelligence. His discovery of a huge black-market ring in Saigon, operated for the most part by military personnel, including a brigadier general, had led to a savage beating and pulping stomping in a vacant warehouse on the Saigon waterfront. His exposé of this vicious racket had not set well with some higher powers. He had been cashiered out of service on a medical discharge.

Disillusioned and bitter, Mark had drifted south from San Francisco after release from the hospital, until he encountered his former football coach at UCLA. When the wizard of the backfield staff learned part of Mark's story and had observed his diminished physical and mental condition, he recommended an unusual cure. Mark was sent to an old friend, Willard Haskins, once head of the Geology Department at USC. In retirement, the professor had constructed a fantastic mansion, a retreat contained within an abandoned borax mine in the Calico Mountains in the California Desert. There Mark began to mend slowly. Then his physical and mental conditioning were undertaken by an aged and ageless Cheyenne medicine chief named David Red Eagle. So startling and rapid had been his improvement, that within months life seemed a magnificent adventure to Mark, something to be desired and held on to. In the course of his therapy, he met and fell in love with Professor Haskins' niece, Donna Morgan.

Together he and Donna searched out his origins. An orphan since the age of seven, Mark had little knowledge of his past or his family history. To the smug satisfaction of David Red Eagle, they discovered that Mark was indeed half Cheyenne Indian, as the old chief had insisted. From then on Mark's training took a different course. Fate did likewise.

During their investigations, Mark and Donna had stumbled onto something that certain dark powers felt they should not know and, if knowing, would be better off dead. A Mafia don named Scarelli put a hit on them both. Donna died and Mark's life was again thrown into turmoil. Out of the crucible of Red Eagle's foundry came a new and different Mark Hardin. Schooled in the ways of the Cheyenne dog soldiers and the martial arts of *Orenda Keowa*, he became a formidable force for ultimate justice. Don Pietro Scarelli, and most of his Mafia "family," died in the blitzkrieg Mark unleashed. It didn't bring Donna back—nothing could—but it did give him and the two old men who backed him one hell of a lot of satisfaction. In the Viking tradition, Mark certainly saw that she had an ample swarm of sidemen to accompany her to Valhalla.

Out of the ashes of that first mission came a force for justice and retribution undaunted by fear, untouchable by bribes and unreachable to destruction. And out of it also came a name, born in the hyperbole of the sensationalist press: THE PENETRATOR. Since then, the Penetrator had undertaken, successfully, fifty-two missions. Each had taken its toll. Friends and lovers had died, men who had begun the fight had grown old. All thoughts of a normal, happy life had been ruthlessly shoved aside in an eternal quest for the righting of wrongs. Until recently, at least.

Time seemed to be running out and he sought a means to reverse the trend.

The Penetrator had gone up against criminal masterminds and corrupt police and politicians, purveyors of filth and the enemies of freedom throughout the world. The price on his head had climbed above the million-dollar mark. And he was tired. In trying to sell himself his idea of a quiet withdrawal from the forefront of vengeance, he reasoned that if he only indulged in the two-year trip, getting to know his new family, it would strongly improve his future chances. After such a time the police, who sought him for innumerable crimes, and the criminals who hated him to the depths of their black hearts and swore to accomplish a vendetta, would consider the Penetrator dead or in hiding. He could freely move about once more, without the constant glance over one shoulder to see if a knife or gun or hurled bomb sought him. By this means, too, he could capture a bit of the happiness so long denied him. Much of this, too, he explained to his wife- and children-to-be on the flight to the Stronghold.

Their arrival created quite a stir. Willard Haskins, a bit stooped by age, embraced Angie and kissed her on one cheek. Then, predictably, he patted the children on their shining towheads and remarked how big and sturdy they were. Karen pouted and Kevin scowled, but the old man didn't seem to notice. For his own part, David Red Eagle had a more formal, though somewhat disconcerting greeting.

"From this day forward, you shall be my

daughter," he told Angie, "as this unruly one is my son." To the twins he added, "Though I am beyond the age to be a grandfather in the true Cheyenne sense, I shall do my best for you. The first thing being to get you some proper clothes."

That left puzzled expressions on the youngsters' faces and Mark winced, visions of moccasins for both, a doeskin dress for Karen and breechclout for Kevin. Red Eagle's notion of proper clothing for children was, he admitted, somewhat dated. They had a late supper together, talking like old friends, then got what sleep the fleeting night allowed.

Early the next morning, the high-ceilinged cavern that housed the black pool rang with the excited shouts and laughter of children, a never-before-heard sound. Mark found the twins there, their clothes in small heaps on the black sand shore. True to his word, Red Eagle had provided for them exactly as expected.

"Hey, Mark!" Kevin shouted, then hesitated in embarrassed uncertainty. "Uh . . . I guess I better get used to calling you Dad, huh? Anyway, c'mon in. It's super!"

"Okay. Only for a while. We're flying to San Diego today."

Mark removed his clothes and dived into the chill water. He surfaced and felt probing tendrils at his ankles, persistent fingers that found their goal and closed about his legs while strong arms encircled him and heaved upward.

In a flash his head went under the surface

and a shouting, giggling pair of tawny youngsters broke through the water. The trio swam
for half an hour, then got out and dried on
big, fluffy terry-cloth towels. Talking with all
the amiable comfort of a real family, they
dressed and climbed up one level for a conge-
nial breakfast.

Slowly a band of thick, black clouds slid over
the face of the moon. Darkness descended on
the Gate of the Sun, and the squared-off, standing pillars around the Plaza of Kalasasaya
faded into dimness. Stillness, accentuated only
briefly by the clatter of a loose stone, filled
the ruins of Tiahuanaco, on the Altiplano of
Bolivia, near the shore of Lake Titicaca. Encouraged by this change, Keith Hovey rose
from where he crouched behind a fallen temple stone and ran silently on tiptoe toward a
new vantage point.

He couldn't see the men who sought him.
His last glimpse of them had been on the
crumbling stairs that ascended the pyramid
of Akapana. Hovey knew they stalked him,
though. He paused and listened in the cover
of one of the andesite monoliths. His heart
pounded, charged by the powerful infusion of
adrenaline that coursed through his veins.
What a hell of a place for Keith Hovey, boy
spook, to be caught in, he thought with a
certain sour cynicism.

A captain in the U.S. Army, Counterintelligence Corps, he had been "on loan" to the
National Security Council for the past two
months. Three weeks of that he had spent in

La Paz, Bolivia, and the environs of Tiahuanaco. And he had found what he had been
sent to look for.

Now the problem remained for him to get
away and carry his information to his contact.
Christ! It was the biggest, most mind-boggling
operation he had ever encountered; in the
files, in the field or in fiction. Leave it to that
son of a bitch, Andropov, to approve such a
scheme. The former head of the KGB, now
turned premier of the Soviet Union, had always seen covert, clandestine operations as
the way to success over the overt, heavy-
handed military adventures like the one cur-
rently stalled in Afghanistan. He would like
this one, all right, and if Project Krisha Mira
got off the ground, it would be such a "Day of
Infamy" that would make the sneak attack on
Pearl Harbor look like a schoolyard game of
fox and geese. Time to move, Hovey, he
decided, jerking himself from his reflections.

Keith Hovey didn't hear the shot, though
the impact of the slug made a hot blossom of
pain in his left shoulder. Small caliber, he
thought irrelevantly, probably from a suppressed TT-33. The 7.62mm slug had enough
behind it, though, to stagger him, and he
lurched into an unseen stone balustrade.

"Over there. I think I hit him," came a
harsh whisper in Spanish.

"Circle around him," a deep voice growled
in the same language, then changed to Russian.
"Yah pat'yeh ohn. Gd'yeh ohn?"

Hovey stuffed his handkerchief under his
shirt in an attempt to staunch the flow of

blood and made a desperate dash to outdistance the men flanking him. In that moment, the half-moon came out from under the cloud cover.

"Voht ohn!" another voice shouted in Russian, then repeated in Spanish, "There he is!"

Bullets screamed from loose stones in a dirt pile and Keith jumped out of the line of fire into a partially excavated drainage canal. He ran along it, legs pounding, while weariness expanded through his body and he felt the sticky trail of blood oozing down his back.

With a final, monumental effort, he reached the outer edge of the pre-Inca ruins. He lifted the sagging, neglected chain-link fabric and crawled under the fence. Half a mile further on his car waited for him. All he had to do was continue to evade the POR gunmen and the deadly agents of the KGB.

From behind him, voices spoke loud and sharp in the night. "Dammit, we've lost him, Comrade Major."

"Oospahkoyt'yes, Constantin! Take it easy," Major Gregor Yatsor told his second in command. "Have Comrade Oquendo send men in cars to search. He can't get far."

Ramón Oquendo flashed a white smile in the moonlight. "It will be a pleasure, comrades, to hunt down the imperialist dog of a spy." He hurried off with his men.

"You see how easy it is, Tulip," Yatsor told Tyolpan through a buzzing laugh, putting heavy emphasis on the KGB agent's code name. "We let these stupid Bolivian peasants do the hard work while we stay here and drink vodka. The American agent will be in our hands within the hour.''

No way! There's no way in hell you will, Keith Hovey raged in his mind while he stumbled over the uneven ground toward his hidden vehicle.

2

KGB CORONARY

Sunlight sparkled in a clear, blue sky, struck bright flashes from the vari-colored southern-California houses and burned away the last traces of mist that frequently shrouded the distant, sawtoothed ridges of the Laguna Mountains. On this most spellbinding of days, San Diego made the perfect place for a marriage. During the three-day wait for the blood-test results, Mark and Angie had taken the twins to Balboa Park, the zoo, Sea World and Scripps Institute. Now the Penetrator waited in an alcove off the nave of St. Therese of the Child Jesus Church on Camino Rico, while Willard Haskins escorted Angie up the aisle.

"I'm nervous," he whispered to David Red Eagle.

"You should be. You have made me nervous enough over the past few days."

"Have I? Yes, I suppose so. I know I didn't make things any easier for the young priest who heard my confession. I haven't exactly been a good churchgoer these past years. I

15

did a lot of 'forgetting,' which didn't make
him happy either."

"Some things cannot be talked about. And
you have done, ah, penance and purification
of a sort in the sweat lodge."

The conversation would have gone on, but
the signal came for Mark to make his appearance. He walked to his place and, at
Angie's side, stood before the altar. The twins
took their proper positions beside Professor
Haskins. The nuptial Mass was conducted by
the assistant rector of St. Therese. Karen and
Angie shed a few joyful tears, Kevin smirked
and wriggled and Mark sweated and worried
that at any moment he would blank out and
forget what he was supposed to say. He mum-
bled the words and nearly dropped the ring
when Red Eagle handed it to him. Colored
beams of sunlight from the stained glass trans-
formed Willard Haskins' features. He looked
unutterably wise and, somehow, beautified.
At first it seemed to Mark that the ordeal
would never be over. Then suddenly he was
being told to kiss the bride and the final blessing was given.

"The Mass is over, you may go," the white-
and-gold-robed priest intoned.

"Thanks be to God."

Afterward, Mark's hand shook when he
signed the church wedding registry and he
nearly dropped the money when he handed it
to the rector.

My God, he thought in discomfort, getting
married is worse than combat. Fortunately,
Mark considered in relief, with so small a

wedding party there would be no reception. Instead the little group got into a single vehicle, a rental limosine, and sped off to the wedding feast Mark had arranged in advance.

Smiling, his dark eyes twinkling behind rimless glasses, their host, Tony Nguyen, met them at the door to Mai Flower Restuarant in the College district of San Diego, near the church. Specializing in Vietnamese cuisine, the tidy establishment nestled in one corner of the Vagabond Motel on El Cajon Boulevard.

"Ah, the Hardin wedding party," Tony greeted. "Please come with me. I have a perfect table for you."

Mark, Angie, the twins, Red Eagle and Willard Haskins followed the dapperly dressed Vietnamese to a large corner booth. There, flowers and a large, white wedding bell in the center of the table awaited them. Soft strains of Southeast Asian music came from hidden speakers. "Please take your seats. Your dinner is already being prepared." Tony's nod indicated the glasses at each place-setting as he went on. "My wife and I are happy to present you with champagne to celebrate. Please feel at home at Mai Flower and enjoy your meal."

With a slight bow, the owner-host departed. In his place came a waiter in black trousers, vest and white shirt. He carried a bottle of Mumms Cordon Rouge in one hand and an ice bucket holding a second bottle in the other. Deftly he put the sweat-beaded container in its stand and poured from the first. Excitement glowed in the eyes of Kevin and Karen

when they hoisted their glasses, smug grins
on their lips. They felt very grown-up and
important at that moment.

"To Mom and Dad," Kevin toasted.

"Long life and happiness," Professor Haskins added, a shaft of late afternoon sunlight
illuminating his gray fringe of curly hair.

"To you, dear," the Penetrator told his over-
joyed wife.

"To all of us, darling," Angie responded.

Red Eagle drained his glass, smacked his
lips and inquired gruffly, "Do they serve buffalo here?"

"Maybe water buffalo, if you ask for it,"
Mark replied in a light, teasing tone.

"Don't be crude," Red Eagle snapped, and
downed a second glass of champagne.

Then the food began to arrive. Large silver
pots, each heated by a small mound of glowing charcoal, were set between each two
persons. Platters of raw vegetables, shrimp
and thin slices of beef came next. Already,
chicken, pork, mushrooms, onions and bok
choy steamed inside the Vietnamese wedding
hot-pots. Rice came, and duck in a hot clay
pot, along with savory lemon-grass chicken,
carafes of chilled French wine and bottles of
fish sauce.

They ate. If only out of self-defense, the six
people scooped food into their mouths and
chewed with utter sybaritic abandon. Then
they had more. Truly a family now, they
laughed and talked their way through the massive banquet, then begged off desert until

Tony came at last with a small, white-iced cake.

"For you," he announced. "May your life together be long and fruitful. And may these beautiful children soon have little brothers and sisters." He departed, laughing and bowing.

"Now for the bad news," Mark announced. "The boat won't be ready and down here from Newport for five days."

A chorus of groans came from Kevin and Karen. Angie glowered at them and they ducked their white-blond heads in contrition. Then Mark went on.

"So, with nothing to do for a while, we'll go to the beach for a couple of days and then fly back north. When the *Bona Fortuna* gets into port, we'll come back and head south to Cabo San Lucas. Then on around the world."

This time even Angie joined in cheering.

Late in the afternon, three days later, David Red Eagle padded silently on moccasin-clad feet to the side of the black pool. A frown if displeasure creased his ancient, lined forehead into deep gullies.

"Mark," he began loudly enough to get over Kevin and Karen's shrieks of delight. "There's a message for you. On the special telephone."

"No. Tell them to forget it. That's all over for now."

"It's Dan. He says it is vital. More than that, a matter of national security, perhaps international. He says he has to talk to you no matter what."

"Oh, hell. I . . . no, dammit. Tell him I'm on

my honeymoon. Tell him to call back in two years or so."

"He says now. Millions of lives are at stake."

"Shit. Okay. Tell him I'll be up in a minute." Mark swam to the narrow shelf of black sand beach and climbed out.

Two other bare, sun-bronzed figures followed him and emerged from the water. Behind them, Angie remained motionless, a stricken expression on her face. Kevin took Mark by the hand, arresting his movement.

"Please don't, Dad. *Please!* Don't go. We . . . we've got to take our trip around the world, right? Don't do it, Dad."

"Please, oh, please!" Karen begged, a thin hint of near-hysteria in her voice.

Mark gently pushed them away and began to dress. Five minutes later he lifted the handset of the scrambled telephone and spoke into it.

"Congratulations, fellah," Dan Griggs offered sincerely.

"My ass, congratulations!" Mark snapped. "At least you could let me enjoy my honeymoon."

"Afraid not. But I am sorry, I didn't know that was what you were about. Look, Buddy, this is important. Damned important. Even knowing you just got married won't change that. Something big is going down in South America. There are so many KGB men down there it looks like a convention on Dzerzenski Square. It might just be the new deal, à la Andropov, but no one at Langley believes it. Satellite photos indicate some sort of hush-

hush activity that involves mighty heavy equipment. There are hints of a massive assault of some sort on the Western Hemisphere.

"That's right, I said the entire hemisphere, not the U.S. or some specific target in Latin America. And get this. Three chemical warfare experts, two from Russia, one from East Germany, have been spotted in La Pax, Bolivia. Right now the thing is so hot, so touchy, that they are calling in all the outside talent they can round up. That means you. Also Sam. She's already on it and you'll be working with her. What they want you to do is go down to La Paz and make contact with a CIC type who has been operating the scene. His agency contact got wiped and the Company folded all their safe houses.

"They put their man down there, it's up to them to get him the hell out," the Penetrator responded in an icy tone.

"Not this time. This is big, the most that KGB has ever undertaken at one time. The Company figures that Andropov's successor pulled out all the stops. No more secrets from their field men. That means all the CIA types have been compromised. It has to be someone from outside the business. You and Sam will be an independent team, you are to get their man and uncover the Soviet operation. When you do, you will have authority to terminate everyone connected. There's no strings on that order. It comes from the highest possible source." The Penetrator had no doubt to whom Dan referred. "Also, from the same source, I have it that you will be offered a presidential pardon, in full, for everything, if you manage to bring this off."

Before Mark could say anything, Dan rushed on. "No. He doesn't know who you are. That won't even be necessary for the pardon. Believe me when I say this. This is what's offerred for what has to be the most critical mission you have ever undertaken. I won't try flag waving on you. But I'm counting on you . . . and so's the Big Guy in the Oval Office. What do you say?"

A long silence followed. "Are you there?" Dan asked anxiously.

"I'm still on. I . . . I have to give it some thought."

"There isn't time."

"Then . . . I . . . oh, goddammit, Dan. I . . . all right. This one time. Then it's quits. For everything and for always."

A prolonged, soulful sigh came across the crackling line. "You restore my faith in my fellowman. Thank you, Mark. Thank you for all of us."

Mark Hardin put down the handset. Unbidden tears filled his eyes. He started at the tormented cry behind him.

"No!" Angie stood in the doorway, her face twisted in anguish. "For the love of God, don't do it, Mark. Please. For me, for the kids, for your own sake. Say no this once."

"I can't, Angie. Too much is riding on it. We talked all this over before, many times. . . ."

"And I said this sort of scene would never happen. You have a right to hold me to my promise. I gave it freely enough. Only . . . it's the first time Kevin and Karen have had a father in nine years. It's . . . it's all so unfair."

"From what Dan Griggs said, we might not have any time together if their suspicions are accurate. Look, I'll call him back, find out details."

Mark quickly dialed. Dan answered on at the second ring. Calmly he went over what he had previously told the Penetrator. He added that an atmosphere of fear hung over those who were aware, both in Washington and the capitals of Latin America.

"When do I have to be in La Paz?"

Dan's reply came in grim-toned words. "Within forty-eight hours. The contact man, a guy you know, by the way, named Keith Hovey, can't hold out much longer. He went in on an emergency request. No time for deep cover. We need to know what he has."

"All right, Dan. Good-bye."

Mark turned to Angie and quickly outlined the situation as given by Dan. Angie's face drained of personal concern and an expression of horror and dismay replaced it.

"Go, then, darling. A pardon is worth a little more risk. I'll manage with the twins. They are rather bright, you know. They'll understand. And . . . and we still have tonight together. After that . . . the whole world. Be careful, my dearest."

A shimmering, much like heat waves seemed to distort the clear, high-country atmosphere along the Prado in downtown La Paz, Bolivia. Keith Hovey knew this could not be so. He had a fever, brought on by his wound, which had become infected. For three days he had been hiding out in a run-down *barrio marginal*, amid the squalor of the less fortunate citizens of this sprawling city. He moved about now with a furtive, animal wariness. Exacerbated by the poison that festered in his bullet-mangled flesh, he lived in expectation of imminent discovery by the opposition and felt an overwhelming sense of betrayal by his own people.

When the young army captain had returned to La Paz near sunrise the morning after his discovery at Tiahuanaco, he had discovered that worse than the wiping of his contact awaited him. The safe house, established by the local station chief, had been dismantled. He had nowhere to wait for a new meet. In the *barrio*, he had established tentative acceptance and an elderly midwife had probed for and removed the bullet, doing, Hovey suspected, more harm than good in the process. The ordeal and his knowledge of the information he carried drove him at last to desperation. He had left his dubious shelter in an attempt to reach the CIA operative at the U.S. consulate.

Hovey located a public telephone and called the number he had been given. After an interminable period of switching from receptionist to secretary to junior diplomat, his man came on the line.

"I've got it," Hovey told him tersely, teeth gritted against the pain. "Everything. When can we meet?"

"We can't. My whole net is under surveillance by the other side. A new contact has been arranged. He will be here within forty-eight hours. His name is Raven. Contact him at the Sucre Palace Hotel, Avenida Sixteen July, number sixteen-thirty-six. The phone is three-five-five-zero-eight-zero. Keep trying until you reach him. And . . . good luck, Hovey."

"I don't . . . don't know if I can hold out that long. I took a hit."

"I'm sorry. Right now, there's nothing more I can do."

Hovey began trying immediately at the hotel. On the first three calls, he received a negative answer. Mr. Raven had not checked in as yet, though a reservation was being held for him. Finally the pain and his deteriorating mental condition forced Hovey to act. He flagged down a taxi and rode to the old Bolivian Colonial-style hotel and appealed directly to the desk clerk.

Again, no luck.

Keith Hovey took a chair in the lobby, watching intently while people came and went. Late in the afternoon, a tall, broad-shouldered man entered with his luggage. Obviously an American, his appearance heightened Hovey's interest. Somehow, even through the fever and delirium, the face of this stranger looked familiar. It brought on fleeting memories of the sweet-sour stench of rotting jungle and the cloying horrors of Vietnam, of a sergeant he had worked with there . . . Holten? Harbin? Then he had it. Sergeant Mark Hardin. That was the name that went with this face. What was Hardin doing there?

More recollections of the young, competent counterintelligence NCO flooded Hovey's mind. Hardin had been newly assigned to CIC, an expert line crosser and a cool, deadly hand with a gun. Would it be safe to pass on to this former buddy the new-gained knowledge that would astound the world? Hovey dismissed the possibility that Hardin could be Raven. He had heard about the big dust-up in Saigon and how Hardin had come into disfavor with certain upper echelons of the military community. Also that he had been severely beaten by members of the black-marketing ring and eventually cashiered out of the army on a medical discharge.

He also had no doubt that Yatsor had managed to track him down. He had already spotted several POR agents lurking around the hotel. Unless he got lucky, he would not live long enough to make his meet with Raven. Worse, if he left the hotel, with the idea of returning later, he would be a dead man before he made a block. Could he trust to Hardin's past loyalties and his present patriotism to make him a safe receptacle for the precious information? He hadn't really the time to worry about it. Covertly he watched Mark Hardin accept his key and walk to the elevator bank. Then Hovey rose, wincing in pain, and walked to the desk.

"That gentleman who just checked in? What is his room number, please?"

The clerk looked momentarily surprised. "Why, señor, that is your friend, about whom you inquired, Señor Raven. He has only this moment checked in. He is in Room two-seven-teen."

"Uh, thank you," Hovey returned, suddenly elated and relieved. So Hardin had stuck with it, eh? He crossed the lobby and took the next car upward.

With growing excitement, Keith Hovey strode along the old, tiled hallway and raised his hand to knock on Mark's door.

3

LAST GASP

Already he missed the comforting warmth of Angie's arms and the noisy energy of the twins, which had brought new life and hope to the Stronghold. Mark began unpacking in his room at the Sucre Palace, placing clothes on hangers and then opening a second metal case that contained a number of deadly items necessary to his business. His arms had been forwarded in a diplomatic pouch and taken from the consulate to a storage locker at El Alto Airport where he picked them up after passing through customs. He wondered when Keith Hovey would contact him and how much the man had changed.

Mark recalled Hovey as a young, hard-charging second lieutenant, fresh out of CIC school, like himself. They had formed a team, running some dangerous ops into the north, bringing torment and destruction to NVA bigshots. They had both treated their risky existence lightly, accepting it all as part of the job. Hovey had a smooth, boyish face, unlined by any of life's harsher realities then.

28

Mark wondered what he would look like after all the years of spooking.

A soft knock sounded on his door. Mark paused, uncertain that it had been at his room. It came again, soft, though persistent. Mark loosened the fit of a High Standard .22 Trophy model automatic he carried in a hip holster and strode to the door. He opened it to a strange, nightmarish sight.

A man, smears of gray at his temples, his face lined with pain and ... something else, anxiety perhaps, slumped against the door post, one hand gripping it while the other attempted to fend off a slender, black, pencil-like object extended at full arm's length by a second individual, a huge bear of a man, who rushed forward, oblivious to everything but his intended target.

In an instant, Mark recognized the tube. A KGB assassination tool. His arm lashed out and he partly deflected the deadly gas gun upward as a thin spray of cyanide fumes poofed out. His other hand darted under his jacket to the butt of the High Standard. He drew the thick-snouted, suppressed weapon and swung it toward the charging man.

Before he could fire, two more men appeared in the hall, near the elevators, both armed with silenced weapons. The huge killer now pinched his nose, or so it seemed, and Mark realized he was sniffing the antidote for the KGB murder device from an amyl-nitrate capsule. The big Russian continued to breathe deeply in an attempt to escape the deadly cyanide fumes while Mark snapped a quick shot at him.

It missed and the Penetrator yanked Keith Hovey into his room. He sent two more silenced rounds at the retreating assassins, one of which found its mark.

A small red spot appeared in a swarthy-faced Bolivian's left eye socket and dark fluid ran from it a moment before a gout of blood. He staggered backward into his companions and they jerked him into the elevator. Mark slammed his door and bolted it. Then he turned to the injured man lying on the floor at his feet.

"Lieutenant? Lieutenant Hovey? Keith can you hear me?"

"M-mark? Is it . . . did I make it?"

"Yeah. For form, I suppose we should go through all the contact crap."

"N-not necessary. Damn, I'd forgotten how fast you move. But . . . no good. I feel dizzy, sick at my stomach. That bastard Yatsor got me with the cyanide. Got . . . to . . . tell you. A-about Krisha Mira. W-with it, the Soviets will have everyone by the balls. T-they are building a transmitter and a huge antenna system. Out . . . out at . . . Oh, God, this stuff eats at your guts. Aah, man, this is my last fucking job. Y-yellow Rain. Look out for Yellow Rain."

"What do you mean, Keith? Where is this? What Yellow Rain?"

"G-gonna dump . . . dump it . . . on us, man. Everyone. I . . . aaaaah!"

"Keith? Keith?" The Penetrator bent low,

gently shaking the American agent. Then Keith's body failed utterly and he voided his bowels and bladder in a final resignation of the flesh husk.

Another KGB coronary carried off, the Penetrator thought bitterly.

He laid Keith's head on the bare tile floor and went to his case of special equipment. From it, he took a compact portable scrambler unit and set it beside the telephone. He lifted the receiver and got the desk.

"I'd like to place a call to the United States, please," he told the operator in Spanish, then gave her the number Dan had provided to contact Samantha Chase.

"It will take a little while, señor. I will call your room when we are ready to put it through."

"Thank you." Mark returned to a grim task. What could he do to dispose of Keith Hovey's body? To haul it out the front door would invite unfortunate questions. Also, the KGB man, Yatsor, knew that Hovey had contacted him. He would have to get another hotel and quickly. He made a quick check of the slim telephone directory and went once more to the phone.

"Three-five-two-one-two-one," he spoke into the mouthpiece.

"*Bueno?* Hotel Crillon," the voice at the other end said crisply.

Mark quickly reserved a room in the name of Roy Bean. Then he returned to his task. He used a sheet to wrap Keith's corpse and had

nearly finished when the phone gave a stri-
dent double ring. *"Bueno?"*

"Mr. Raven?"

"This is he."

"This is your friend at the consulate. How
did you find your room?"

"Busy," the Penetrator answered tersely. "I
met the man you wanted me to talk to. He
didn't say much. Had a heart attack. You
know the kind. Got a look at the other side,
too."

"My, you have been busy."

"Like I said. Can you do something about
my present problem?"

"In an hour or so."

"Make it faster than that. I have to take
new accommodations."

"I understand. We'll get right on it. Now,
when can I meet you?"

"You won't be doing that. Remember the
terms of my job interview? I will do this alone,
my way."

An Andean chill tinged the CIA man's words.
"You had better be successful."

"I will be. Let me know what you come up
with for this little problem."

"Soon."

The line went dead. Before Mark could kneel
beside Hovey's body again, the bell sounded
once more.

"Ready with your call to Florida."

"Thank you."

"Hi, guy," Sam's voice came over the fading,
drifting line. "Everything okay?"

"Far from it," the Penetrator told her through

the scrambler unit. "Our boy got taken out by the other side. Died in my room. He mentioned some nasty stuff before he went, though. Yellow Rain. You checked out on that?"

A pause came. "Yes, some. Where? Can you tell me that?"

"Not for sure. Not yet."

"I'm coming down. I can catch a LAB flight out of Miami tomorrow morning."

"Good. I'll meet you. And, Sam, be careful. We've got one player out of the game now."

"Cover your own ass, fellah. You're the one hanging out there. Is ... is Gregor Yatsor involved?"

"That's the name Hovey gave me."

"Then be specially careful for me, lover. He's a mean one."

"I will. See you tomorrow."

4

ROOF OF THE WORLD

Two waiters, their black vests unbuttoned and food stains from the noon rush on their white, half aprons, stood at the service bar in the rear of the Verona Restaurant exchanging idle comments. The midafternoon siesta time had arrived and most of the staff had already departed. They gave only casual, disinterested glances when Gregor Yatsor and Constantin Tyolpan entered and took a booth to one side. A moment later, Ramón Oquendo and Luis Torreos rounded the corner from Calle Colón and walked into the café.

"I am sorry, señores, we are not serving meals now," one waiter informed the four men.

"That is all right," Yatsor declared. "Just bring us some tea, please."

When the man complied and withdrew, Yatsor dumped a large quantity of sugar into his steaming glass and stirred thoughtfully. At last he leaned forward, his voice tinged with tight urgency. "The time is drawing near, comrades. Within the next ten days, your chosen representatives will be the de jure government of Bolivia. I needn't stress the importance of everything going according to plan."

"So soon?" Oquendo returned. He smoothed the lapel of his expensive, hand-made suit and wrinkled his leathery forehead with a frown. The hard cruel slash of his mouth, a legacy of his half–Chacobo Indian ancestry, firmed and he licked his lips with a small strip of tongue. "We have waited the day since the glorious beginnings with El Ché," he breathed out in satisfied contemplation. Then a harsh bark of laugh sprang from deep in his throat.

"Hardly did we expect it to come almost overnight!"

"I can assure you it is real, Comrade Oquendo," Yatsor purred. "The party here in Bolivia has for too long sought its guidance from the Marxist elements of the Third World. It is only the Soviet Union who can bring the ultimate victory. Our technology, coupled with proper Marxist-Leninist thought is undefeatable. What I need to know is whether the men to form the new government have been brought here to La Paz?"

"Here? The capital is Sucre."

"The constitutional capital, yes. But we all know the real power lies in La Paz. When Krisha Mira is activated, the decadent imperialist lackeys in Sucre will be ordered to dissolve their government. The new one will be announced from here on Radio Illimani and Channel Seven, once your POR forces seize them from the government." Yatsor grew impatient. "This is nothing new. We have been over it any number of times. When will you have the men here?"

"Why, by tomorrow, if you wish, comrade."

"No. Five days from now. There is no need to rush this. The major concern of all of us is secrecy. I am authorized to inform you that the possibility exists that if anything at all is exposed about Project Krisha Mira, there is a chance that the Americans may retaliate with a nuclear strike. You can be certain they won't be firing missiles at Bolivia. Protection of Mother Russia must be the foremost consideration . . . of all of us."

"I understand, comrade," Oquendo replied, his flippant manner wilting under the hot glare of the Soviet agent.

"I have a question, comrade," Torreos interjected. "Since I will be leading the attack force on the government-owned broadcast facilities, how much time will I have to alert my troops and move into position?"

"Twelve hours at the most. Perhaps less."

Torreos studied the Russian with deep-set, piercing eyes that glowed from his gaunt, skull-like face. "That doesn't leave much leeway. I have some elements to move from the jungles of the Beni district and from the Santa Cruz and Potosí."

"Start them now," Tyolpan suggested.

Torreos brightened, his light-compected, Spanish features relaxing. "Yes. I could do that. Could they stay out near the project?"

"No," Yatsor declared finally. "On the opposite side of town from us. Security, comrade, remember that."

"Certainly, Comrade Yatsor."

"Speaking of security," Yatsor went on while he looked around the restaurant. The midafternoon coffee and sweet-bread customers had begun to fill the place. "We had better continue this discussion at the project site."

Tyolpan threw some coins on the table and rose with the others. They left the restaurant to take their separate ways to Tiahuanaco.

Impatient that nothing had happened through the long afternoon, Mark Hardin picked up the telephone again and called the CIA contact at the consulate. When the man answered, his words were testily given, barely polite.

"We're working on it," he curtly announced.

"Work harder. Get a laundry truck or some tradesman's van. Come to the service entrance and on up to my room. Take your man out in a basket or something."

A dry chuckle came from the other end. "Where did you get that old chesnut? Been watching James Bond movies?"

"I don't want the locals finding a corpse in my room," the Penetrator went on, ignoring the sarcasm. "And I don't think you want that either. I'm leaving here in fifteen minutes, so do something, even if it's wrong." He hung up before the CIA man could respond. Don't lose your temper, he cautioned himself. Grimly he continued packing.

Ten minutes later a knock sounded at Mark's door.

He went to it and opened up cautiously, his High Standard in his right fist. A man in a white uniform stood there, a large laundry hamper beside him. On his chest a small embroidered patch read, *"Limpiaduria La Capital."*

"You had a pickup for us, señor?" The man was an American; Mark was sure of that. His looks and accent, though, were pure Bolivian.

"Yes. Come on in."

Once inside, with the door closed, Mark showed the man Keith Hovey's body. "So your boss went for this one, did he?" he asked amused.

"No one came up with anything better," the CIA agent responded with a slight trace of Chicago accent to his English. "And you didn't give us a hell of a lot of time."

Mark helped load the cadaver into the hamper. "Sorry about that. Now, for what Hovey told me." Quickly the Penetrator outlined the sketchy information the dead American agent had imparted. He concluded with a personal observation. "The Russians call it Project Krisha Mira. That means 'Roof of the World.' I've heard of it somewhere before."

"Yes. So have I. Well, we're certainly at the roof of the world here in La Paz."

"When I was pulled in on this, the thinking went that more territory is involved than Bolivia. What is it? Orbital missiles? That transmitter and an antenna system have got me thinking."

"What worries me more is your mention of Yellow Rain. The Soviets have the largest chemical service forces of any army in the world. The bastards are using it in Afghanistan. Yellow Rain is more or less an umbrella code designation for a series of deadly chemical agents. Terror is an effective weapon in the proper hands. The toxins in the Yellow Rain group kill quickly and hideously. The Soviets have more delivery systems than we have protective gear types or detector devices.

"Since the 1972 Biological Warfare Convention, which the Soviets signed, but no more honor or adhere to than any other treaty they've ever signed, there is evidence that they can cause a wide range of diseases as well as countermeasures for them. The Sverdlovsk incident in seventy-nine is a good indicator of that."

"What happened in that one?" Mark inquired, intrigued now by this horrifying form of barbarism.

"A strain of airborne anthrax wiped out a lot of people and killed off some animals. The Soviets claimed it was from 'bad meat.' Our best estimates, based on available information, indicate that a biological warfare center near the city had an accident. The same sources believe that the Soviets have produced virulent strains of the plague, cholera, anthrax, tularemia, lassa fever, ebola fever and marburg fever. The dissemination of these falls under the umbrella of Yellow Rain, although not technically the same as the nonreproductive trichothecene toxins that first bore that name and are being used against Afhgan civilians and noncombatants.

"The thing that makes it all so terrifying is that we, all of the Free World, are helpless to do anything about the employment of these agents short of a massive preemptive nuclear strike that would destroy the Soviet Union. No one in their right mind wants to bring down that sort of thing. It wouldn't destroy the world, but it could put man back to the Stone Age in a generation."

"So in the meantime we simply close our eyes and ears and let the Soviets get away with it?"

"That's why all the flap about Krisha Mira. We don't know what the Russians are up to. But if there is the slightest possibility that they intend to employ chemical or biological agents in any way against the West, every person connected to the project must be terminated."

"That's what I am supposed to be here for," the Penetrator told him.

The agent's eyes opened slightly, then hooded over in surprised and worried speculation. Who could this man be? Even looking at him he felt a threatening aura of death emanating from the hawk-beaked face and powerful-shouldered body. An involuntary shudder climbed his spine.

Deep in the ground, under the Akapana pyramid at Tiahuanaco, Gregor Yatsor sat behind his desk, a glass of vodka in his pudgy, hamlike left fist. He toasted the other men in the room. *"Zavashe nostrovnia, Tovarichi!* Here we are, beneath the pitiful remains of a vain people's attempt to elevate the opiate of the people to the status of divinity. How fitting that this *temple*"—his voice grew larded with scorn—"be the place from which the decadent West shall at last be destroyed and the new world of Marxist purity be brought into being." He turned, smiling, to a white-smocked scientist at one side of the room.

"Krisha Mira will kill millions, eh Dr. Moller? But that is of no importance. We have no need of the slaves. The world is overcrowded as it is. We'll be doing a service. Don't you see it that way?"

The gray-haired, crew-cut scientist studied the huge Russian agent. He despised the KGB, thought them even more brutish animals than Himmler's crew. Life had been so much better under the Nazis, he reflected. Even Auschwitz had seemed a kindergarten compared to the Gulag. He had taken specimens from both places for his experiments. Unfortunately he found himself often agreeing with this huge bear of a man for other than defensive reasons. He ran long, aesthetic-looking fingers through the burrlike fringe of his scalp and sighed.

"Yes, Comrade Yatsor. The world is over populated. It is unruly and disordered. Marxism represents order. Therefore what we do here is to improve the world situation through proper order."

Yatsor laughed and slapped his free hand on a thick thigh. He gulped from the vodka and wiped tears from his eyes. "You sound like my party theoretician at the Leningrad Institute. There is no one more dedicated than a convert and you Nazis make the most dedicated converts of all. We thank you, Comrade Doctor, for your inspiring rhetoric. Everything is on schedule in your department?"

Moller nodded. "The vials of toxins and other biological agents are ready to be distributed to the launch sites. As to Blue-X and Agent Pakaznoy—or the Flash as the Americans call it—they will be ready when needed. Once the biological agents and chemicals, including blister agents, blood agents and nerve gas, are released in the target cities from the low-altitude cruise missiles, the population will have from one-half minute to twenty-four hours to live. Barring meteorological difficulties such as rain, high winds or snow, the effect should be total. Everyone within five miles of the release point will die."

"Thank you, Comrade Doctor. Now, what of the missiles?" Yatsor asked Boris Balnoy.

A soft smile stole over Balnoy's features. Young for his position as computor programmer for the entire Krisha Mira Project, he felt a certain justifiable pride and determination to be successful. The freckles on his broad cheekbones stood out against the pallor of his skin and seemed to writhe when he spoke.

"The program for all launch trajectories has been completed, inserted into the banks and tested. We are ready to activate a test launch at any time, Comrade Director Yatsor. The missiles are all in place and waiting to be fueled."

"Fine. Excellent. How about the transmitter and the antenna system, Constantin?" Yatsor asked of his second in command.

"Comrade Eskraye assures me they will be ready ahead of schedule, which is less than five days from now. Perhaps in as little as three."

"Excellent. Comrad Balnoy, I think you can order the start of fueling for the first test launch."

"At once, comrade."

"Comrades! Within days now, the entire West will be prostrate, the major cities disease- plague- and chemical-ridden wastelands and their governments in the hands of loyal party members who have long waited the day to take over. This time, through the genius of our courageous premier, Comrade Andropov, the Soviet Union cannot be stopped."

5

VIOLENT ENCOUNTER

Dawn came crisp and cold in the high, thin Andean air. If it hadn't been for his frequent flights in the unpressurized Mooney, the Penetrator knew, he would be like most first-time visitors to La Pax. Those accustomed to the lowlands found themselves gasping for breath, their hearts laboring to provide oxygen from the rarefied air and compelled to take frequent drafts from portable oxygen bottles until their bodies acclimated. Impatience gnawed at him. Samantha's flight would not arrive until midafternoon. He felt time stealing the tactical advantage from him.

So far he had killed a Bolivian Communist and made his involvement known to the KGB station chief, Gregor Yatsor. He had moved from the Sucre Palace, wisely not taking the room he had reserved at the Crillon. He selected yet another hotel, the Gloria, across the street from the House of Culture on Calle Potosí. As further precaution he had used another name. This maneuver, hopefully, would restore some of his lost advantage of surprise.

44

Still, he felt helpless until Sam arrived and they laid out a plan of action.

Room service turned out to be a risky proposition for breakfast, so at noon Mark left his quarters to dine at La Fontana Coffee Shop in the Plaza Hotel. He took with him a light load of weapons—a Guardfather spring-loaded spike, his .22 High Standard with full sleeved-barrel suppressor and a small aerosol canister of an incapacitating agent far more powerful than mace—all he felt he would need in the event of trouble on the streets.

After working his way through an enormous, savory sandwich of charbroiled *parrillada*, he made arrangements for transportation. At Oscar Crespo Maurice Rent-a-Car, he obtained a Toyota Land Cruiser. Outside the cities, Bolivia had few paved roads and Mark accepted the necessity of a four-wheel-drive vehicle. His international driver's license and automobile-club cards made the rental procedure simple. He pocketed the paperwork and drove down Calle Mayor Carranza toward the "street of many names." When the street signs told him that Avenida Perez Velasco finally became Avenida Montes, Mark had his bearings, knowing that the new highway to El Alto Airport lay not far beyond. He also knew that he had picked up a tail.

The Penetrator drove sedately along the modern freeway until it had passed beyond the poorer barrios of the city and then skirted the Altiplano for the brief, mile-long journey to El Alto. With skill and tenacity, the car following him remained an unobtrusive distance behind.

At the airport, Mark steered his Land Cruiser into the parking lot. He selected a space that left three empty slots on each side and one in front of him. He climbed from behind the wheel and locked the door. He heard the whine of the VW engine a second before it rushed down on him and screeched to a halt. Three men, all armed, leaped out.

In a blur of speed, the Penetrator's right hand went to the butt of his High Standard. His thumb released the safety as he brought the bulky barrel into the open. His left yanked the canister of CS from the case on his belt.

The nearest man's feet slapped noisily on the paving when he lurched to a sudden stop as droplets of the incapacitant struck his face and eyes. He gasped violently, as though suffering a heart attack, and fell to the ground. His comrades pressed on.

Mark took a quick shot with the High Standard, and the bullet moaned off the curved steel roof of the Volkswagen. A knife split the air inches from his face and he released a long spray with the CS. The knife artist uttered a strangled groan and turned away, doubled over and clawing at his eyes. That opened a clear field of fire to the third assassin.

The High Standard chuffed silently and two poison-filled .22 hollowpoints zipped across the short distance to his chest. The slugs struck bone and expanded, releasing the deadly compound from their wax-sealed cavities. By this time the first assailant had recovered suffi-

ciently to bring up his Mexican-made Obregon
.45 and blast the silence of the battle with a
sharp report.

A loud clang assaulted the Penetrator's ears
in the same instant that intense pain, followed by a wave of numbness, radiated up
his arm from his hand. The slug had struck
the fat tube of the silencer and wrenched the
piece from Mark's hand. It fell to the ground.
Instinct sent him in a dash to the far side of
the killers' car while he shook his hand in an
attempt to restore feeling and control. The
Penetrator groped in his shirt pocket and, when
the gunman came after him, drew his Guardfather. He still couldn't rely on it for a thrust,
so he snapped his right hand up and back,
releasing the locked-open spike in a backhand
throw.

The needle point of the Guardfather bit into
flesh in the notch at the base of the man's
throat and slid deeply inside. He forgot about
the Obregon in his fist and dropped it so that
both hands could claw at the fiery agony in
his trachea. The Penetrator took a step forward and used the palm of his hand in a
teisho stroke that drove the slender shaft of
steel in to the hilt. His enemy had already
begun a death dance when he turned away to
deal with any of the others who remained in
the fray.

No one moved. And nobody as yet had been
attracted by the gunshot. He walked to the
second CS victim and knelt beside him.

Mark roused the man, then drew him upward with a rough jerk on his hair. "Who sent you after me?" he demanded in Spanish.

"Camarada Oquendo of the Partido Obrero Revolucionario," came the reply.

"What was your mission?"

"To . . . to kill you."

"Where is Oquendo?"

"I do not know."

Without comment, the Penetrator rose, retrieved his High Standard and returned. He went down on one knee and put the muzzle an inch from the POR assassin's left ear. Realization of Mark's intention filled the man with terror and he cried out pitiously.

"No! Please, no. I am a prisoner of war. You must . . ."

The Penetrator fired a single shot.

Now to tidy up, Mark thought. He crossed to the VW and drove it into an empty slot. Then he returned to the area of carnage and dragged the corpses to the car one by one. Carefully he arranged them in sitting positions, cleaned and pocketed his Guardfather and locked the doors. He turned away and headed for the doorway that indicated arrivals on Lloyd Aereo Boliviano.

"Hey, good-lookin'," the Penetrator greeted Samantha Chase when she walked out of the customs area two hours later.

"Hey, yourself. The altitude must be good for you. You are in terrific shape."

Mark took her luggage and started toward the door. "We had a little excitement while I was waiting. Someone found three dead men in a car in the parking lot."

Sam's eyes widened and went a bit soft in worry. "Oh, Mark. Did you . . . ?"

He nodded and walked out into the weak highland sunlight. "A trio of gunmen from the Partido Obrero Revolucionario," he explained when they got clear of the cluster of arriving passengers. "Everyone is in on the act. The KGB hit Hovey and made a try for me already. Now this. Who next? Just what the hell did you get into, kid?"

"I'll explain it all later. Right now I can hardly wait to get to your hotel room and into bed."

Mark stopped, still several strides from the Land Cruiser. "Uh . . . Sam . . . for, ah, security reasons I got you a room in another hotel."

"Okay. So we use my bed. Once we get rolling on this thing there won't be a lot of time for that sort of thing and . . . well, I've been needing you a whole lot lately, you gorgeous hunk."

Mark winced and tried to frame the words. "Ah . . . there's another, ah, reason, Sam. You see . . . I . . . well, I'm married now. I got married to Angie, you don't know her, but anyway we were married three days before I took this mission."

"Married?"

"God, sometimes I hate that word," the Penetrator responded in frustration and embarrassment.

"You? Married? Then Dan wasn't shitting

me when he said you were going to call it quits?"

"Nope. After this job is over."

They proceeded to the Land Cruiser and Mark put Sam's bags in the back. When he turned to open the front door for her, she took his arm, possessively, and snuggled up, her cheek on his shoulder.

"Lord, how I envy the girl, whoever she is."

When the cream-tan Land Cruiser pulled out of the parking area, Mikhail Koretsa nodded to the swarthy Chacobo Indian from POR who drove their Jeep Ranger.

"That's the one. Follow him and don't be seen. When we reach the right spot, we will take them."

"Sí, Camarada Koretsa."

"Yes," the KGB agent said aloud in self-satisfaction. "We must find a most unusual and original way to kill them both."

6

DEADLY RIDE

"Here we are, the best in town," the Penetrator cheerfully informed Sam when he pulled the Land Rover to a stop at the main entrance of the Plaza Hotel on the Paseo del Prado.

"This looks expensive," Samantha Chase objected.

"It is. You might as well have the best, though, if Uncle is picking up the check, no? Seriously, I picked it because the security is good, the door locks all work and you get a superb view of the city from the Utama Restaurant on the top floor."

Sam stifled the beginnings of a giggle. "You sound positively giddy. Married life must agree with you."

"It does. Believe me. Let's get you checked in, then we can go over this mission a little more thoroughly."

"Anything you say."

Mark's advance reservation made check-in easy. Since it was siesta time, the bellboys were all off, an apologetic bell captain explained. He would be glad to take the lady's luggage if she wished. Sam declined. She and Mark entered the elevator and began the ascent through the tall central tower of the Plaza.

Between the eleventh and twelfth floors, the car suddenly came to a stop with a harsh jolt that sent giddy, seesaw vibrations through the creaking structure.

"W-what is it, Mark?" Sam asked.

"Could be a power failure. They are frequent enough in Bolivia that most modern buildings have auxiliary generators. No doubt the Plaza does. It should kick in any second now."

Instead, faint vibrations of another nature began to transmit themselves along the suspending cable into the body of the car. The elevator gave a lurch and footsteps sounded on the roof of the lift.

"Repair men?" Sam inquired.

"Could be," Mark responded cautiously. He reached under his coat and drew his silenced High Standard.

"Hurry with that trapdoor, Miguel," a voice above whispered harshly in Spanish, "so I can throw this grenade."

As quickly as he could trigger them, the Penetrator sent six rounds through the ceiling of the car. "Trouble," he advised Sam dryly.

A man screamed, a short, piercing cry, and fell heavily onto the roof. The car yoyoed precariously while the trapdoor flew open and two men leaped inside, weapons in their hands.

One short, swarthy killer lunged toward Samantha with a long-bladed, cheap copy of a Persian horsehead knife glittering in his right fist. He aimed the tip for a blow to her heart. He failed to reach the easy-looking target.

Sam spoiled his day with an *uchi ude uke* inside forearm block, augmented by the presence of a Cold Steel Urban Skinner. The moment the Bolivian Red's arm and blade cleared her body, she snapped her left arm forward in a modified *furi zuki* flare punch that drove the three-inch stainless-steel push dagger into her attacker's right deltoid muscle.

He grunted in agony and the horsehead dropped from nerveless fingers. In the same instant, Sam wrenched the blade free, aided by the cutout socket in the Urban Skinner. It came free with a sucking sound and she swung the razor edge toward his throat while driving a *uchi hiza giri* inside knee blow to his groin.

Before the POR assassin could bend over from the blinding pain exploding in his testicles, steel met flesh again and smoothly sliced into his neck. Sam put more pressure behind her slashing motion and the push dagger opened his carotid artery and jugular. Sam shoved him back and away, so that the growing fountain of blood did not spray on her and turned to see how Mark fared with his man.

A jagged cut ran across the back of the Penetrator's right hand, not deep, but painful enough to have caused him to drop his High Standard. He grappled bare-handed with his opponent in an attempt to wrest the knife from his hands.

Sam thought to move in and take the Bolivian in the kidney with her Urban Skinner, but in the closer quarters of the elevator car her luggage and the corpse at her feet hampered her movement. Stymied, she stood back while the killer tried a backhand swing with the knife.

His motion allowed the Penetrator to break free of the choking fingers that grasped his throat. He blocked the slash with a *nagashi uke* sweeping right-hand block and a *yon hon nukite* spear hand thrust into his attacker's floating ribs.

"Unngh!" The POR assassin gasped and the Penetrator felt the elastic bones give beyond their endurance and break. Hurting, though still game, he tried to rip upward into Mark's belly.

Mark stopped it with a *gedan ude uke* forearm block. The Bolivian tried to leap backward and slammed against the wall. Mark used the respite to bend down and retrieve his High Standard in a left-handed grip. His opponent saw the weapon and his mouth pulled into a startled "Oh!" a moment before Mark shot him twice in the stomach.

The would-be killer developed a sagging, doubtful expression, and as the poison in the bullet tips spread through his nervous system he sagged to the floor.

"I think I heard another one moving around on top," Samantha whispered to Mark.

He holstered his High Standard and boosted himself upward in the open hatchway. From the corner of his eye he caught a blur of motion and dropped below the rim of the trapdoor a fraction of a second before a foot swished past, its owner intent on kicking Mark's head into the room beyond the elevator shaft.

This maneuver had a distinct disadvantage, which the POR assassin discovered immediately. Swaying on the rocking car, he lost his balance and fell to the roof. The Penetrator seized the advantage to swing up to the outer platform and close with his enemy.

Each movement had to be carefully gauged; Mark's footing on the supported car was so unstable that every lunge threatened to override the safety brakes. The killer tried another kick and missed. An involuntary whimper escaped from his throat when the elevator slipped downward a fraction of an inch. Then the Penetrator grabbed his shirtfront and hauled him upright.

A big fist smashed into the man's face, and for an instant spotty lights cavorted behind his eyes. He managed an underhand knuckle-joint punch that rocked the Penetrator back and gave him time to come to his feet.

Nimble as a mountain cat, the Penetrator sprang upward and blocked another attack. With so perilous a footing, kicks were definitely out. When the man came at him again, he took a defensive horse stance and unleashed a *morote zuki* U-punch that slammed his opponent back against the wall of the shaft.

Suddenly the elevator motor hummed to life and the car began to ascend toward the turning mechanism two floors above. Small patters of dust-crusted grease rained down on them and the Penetrator could see the revolving wheels draw nearer at an ever-increasing speed.

"Good news, Comrade Yatsor," Ramón Oquendo announced when he entered the small cubicle that served the KGB station chief as an office. "Your man, Comrade Koretsa, has reported in. He has located the American agents and is directing my men in their disposal in an elevator car at the Plaza Hotel."

Gregor Yatsor allowed himself one of his infrequent smiles. "That is good news. If your men are competent enough, they might carry it off this time." Conscious of the touchy nature of these Latin American comrades with their bourgeoise concept of *machismo*, he hurried to make himself clear. "No, no, I am not insinuating that you and your comrades are incompetent. Merely that you had singularly bad luck at El Alto. With Mikhail in charge, they should be more fortunate."

"The men at the airport were from the jungles, two only a generation removed from tribal life. I chose urban guerrillas who are on familiar territory. You will be pleased with the results, comrade. That I promise you."

"Excellent, Comrade Oquendo. Now, if you will excuse me, I have work to do."

After Oquendo departed, Yatsor returned his attention to large aerial maps of South America. His finger rested on Rio de Janeiro. Yes, Rio . . . most definitely, he thought. Population over eight million. And it gives our navy easy access to the harbor that way. Where else? he contemplated. Buenos Aires, Santiago, Sucre, Lima, of course, Bogotá, Caracas. That should be enough here. Now for Central America. Enough cities will die to throw the entire West into blind panic. And ... they won't dare retaliate when they don't know how it happened or what we used. The specter of the carnage soon to come brightened his day.

Eyes white and round in fear at the realization that his own death approached, the Bolivian Communist became reckless. He lunged at the Penetrator, uncaring of the painful blows to his head and shoulders. He sought to crush the man in his powerful arms. Mark pivoted gracefully and smashed his assailant's nose with a *uraken* back-fist. Only a few feet separated the struggling men from crushing crossbeams and the spinning cable reel above.

The Penetrator drew his High Standard and shot the POR terrorist in the temple. Instantly Mark dropped through the open trapdoor a brief fraction of a second before the car jolted to a stop, the steel I-beams only two inches from the roof.

"Let's see if we can get this thing to go down," Mark, appearing unruffled from his ordeal, suggested to Sam.

Before he could act on his words, the doors opened. In front of them stood a tall, slender European with a Soviet Makarov pistol in his left fist. He motioned with the muzzle, a menace and an order.

"Come out," he curtly told them.

The Russian agent apparently did not see the thick-barreled High Standard in the Penetrator's hand. Mark brought it up and shot Mikhail Koretsa low in the abdomen. His last two rounds had been standard solid-point bullets, with no poison. Koretsa staggered backward and started to fire the Makarov. Mark shot him a second time, in the left kneecap.

Comrade Koretsa went down with a moan that grew into a high-pitched, nearly silent whine of agony. Samantha kicked his pistol away and they met over the body.

"Into the elevator with him," the Penetrator decided. "We haven't much time. We go down two floors to your room, stash the bodies and question this one. Then we have to get out of this hotel."

Sam nodded grimly. "Somehow the thought of staying here has lost a lot of its appeal." She helped Mark drag Mikhail Koretsa into the car and punched the button.

Obediently, the elevator performed its normal function this time. Sam took her luggage and opened the door to her room. She returned and helped the Penetrator drag the corpses into her suite. They returned for the groaning Koretsa and hurried him along to a couch in the living room of the two-room apartment.

"Get a cold washcloth, Sam," the Penetrator instructed. She left the room and Mark turned to their prisoner. He bent low at the sound of rapid crunching, like someone eating hard candy. A faint odor of almonds rose from Koretsa's lips.

Mikhail Koretsa thought briefly of his dishonor at the hands of these American bourgeois enemies. He thought of his home and his family. Then he thought of the triumph that would soon be delivered to his beloved Soviet Union. Then he had a fleeting moment of superstitious peasant fear. . . . What if . . . what if there really were a God? Then he thought of nothing as the powerful poison in his suicide pill took total effect.

7

INTERLUDE

"Shit!" the Penetrator exploded with an oath. "We lost him, Sam. He took a suicide pill."

"Oh, hell, now we'll never learn what he knew."

"Enough, you can be sure. And his boss has to be Yatsor. He smells of KGB." Mark began to go through Koretsa's clothing. Among the items he located were a Soviet passport and credentials identifying him as the agricultural attaché with the Soviet cultural mission. A common KGB cover. The papers didn't identify him by his real name but as Anatole Borodin.

"What do we do with . . . these?" Sam inquired, eyeing the bodies.

"The Bolivians we can dump down the laundry chute in the maid's pantry. This one . . . I don't know."

"I have an idea."

"What is it?"

"The local authorities are going to raise hell over finding a foreigner's body, right? Particularly one with diplomatic immunity.

So what we do is create an incident that will be so embarrassing to the Soviets that they themselves will put on pressure to hush it all up."

"Like what?"

"Our friend Anatole there had an illicit affair going ... with a mysterious American woman who disappears."

A smile split Mark's face into horizontal lines of merriment. "I think that might work, kid. Let's get going."

Quickly they undressed the dead Russian and sprawled him on the bed, which Mark industriously rumpled. Sam put a thick layer of lipstick on and smeared Koretsa's shirt collar with a light brush of her lips, then kissed him soundly on the neck and one cheek, squinting her eyes tightly shut. From the small, built-in bar in the living room, the Penetrator took a bottle of Calvados brandy and poured a little into the dead man's sagging mouth.

"Get me a couple of glasses. Wear gloves," he ordered Sam. She hurried to comply.

The Penetrator filled the glasses with liquor and pressed the corpse's fingers around one. He then instructed Sam to press her lips to the second.

"Now," he announced with satisfaction, "the stage is set."

A few seconds with a set of lockpicks opened the maid's pantry. Mark retrieved a rolling hamper and trundled it to Sam's room.

"Help me load the two POR boys into this," he told Sam.

Together they dumped them down the laundry chute.

"Now, hang a 'do not disturb' sign on the door, lock it and we'll leave by a back route," he instructed, taking a last look around Sam's suite.

"I'm going to hate leaving all this luxury."

"Not to worry. We'll find you something nice."

Half an hour later, the Penetrator prepared to leave Sam's new room in the Hotel Libertador, on Calle Obispo Cardenas. Sam came to him and stood on tiptoe. She kissed him lightly on the lips.

"You owe me a dinner for all this," she challenged.

"Done. I'll pick you up at eight for a drink, then on to an authentic Bolivian feast."

"Where are we going?" Sam asked when they left a small lounge and entered a taxi.

"Restaurante Naira," the Penetrator replied, instructing the cabbie at the same time. "It's supposed to have the best in Bolivian food at less than exorbitant prices."

Their driver braked in front of number 161 Calle Sagárnaga a few minutes later. Mark allighted and helped Sam out, then handed the taxi operator a fifty-peso note. They entered the restaurant and seemed to have stepped backward in time to medieval days.

Long, wooden trestle tables with place settings made of locally produced pottery filled the room. Dark, smoke-stained beams crossed the ceiling and the walls appeared to be native stone. The maître d' escorted them to a table and bowed himself away, his place taken by a crisply uniformed waiter.

"We'll each have a *pisco* sour," Mark ordered. "And we would like a wine with dinner."

"The local vintages are most excellent, señor."

"Fine. May I see the list?"

A black-sleeved arm with a snowy, lace-edged cuff produced the stiff folder instantly. "I will bring your drinks."

"What do we do now?" Mark asked. "The KGB seems to have all the cards."

"You've been here longer than I. You tell me."

"I think we have no choice but to follow up the slim lead Hovey gave me before he died. We go to Tiahuanaco."

"Right out there with the Soviets?"

"In the daytime, to start with. All the tourists do."

"When?"

"Tomorrow. I want to get this cleaned up quickly."

"And get back to the wife and kiddies?"

Mark frowned. "Sarcasm doesn't fit you, Sam."

Water filled Sam's eyes and she wore a contrite expression. "I wasn't being a cynic, Mark; I was being a bitchy, jealous woman. Forgive me?"

"You know I do."

Their drinks arrived and they sipped the grape-brandy sours. Mark took a hand-rolled Bolivian cigar from his jacket pocket and lighted it. After a few satisfying puffs, their conversation resumed.

"Hovey seemed anxious to get the information across to me, as though there might not be much time before the Soviets implemented this Project Krisha Mira."

"Then we go tomorrow," Sam agreed.

"Do you wish to order now, señor, señora?"

"Yes. We'll start with an appetizer plate of *empenadas salteñas*. Then the *picante de pollo, muy picante, por favor*. Then the *laguna Titicaca truca*."

When the waiter departed, Sam turned a puzzled expression on the Penetrator. "What is all that stuff?"

"You've had dim sum? Well, the *empenadas salteñas* are sort of like that; small, spicy pastry turnovers of beef, eggs, olives, peas, potatoes, onions and peppers. The *Picante de Pollo* is chicken in a really strong garlic and chili gravy. And of course fresh trout from Lake Titicaca."

"My God, all that? I'll founder."

"No you won't. You eat like three people anyway."

The *Empenadas* arrived promptly. They proved to be crisply fried and salty on the outside, steamy hot and savory within. Sam crunched her teeth into the first one with delicate precision, then exclaimed aloud.

"Why, these are marvelous! I can hardly wait for the next course."

Salad and soup came before the chicken. Once they had finished off, drinking a bottle of Chilean *unduraga* white wine with dinner, they leaned back, replete and a bit droopy-eyed. Sam took a pack of Camel filters from her purse and lit one.

"Have you been following the recent Soviet violations of international law in Afghanistan?"

"Not much, Sam."

"Considering our Marxist-loving media, it's no wonder few people know about it. Even the noble, paternalistic United Nations failed to find what they called, 'significant evidence of any violations of the 1925 Geneva Protocol or the seventy-two Biological Warfare Convention.' Naturally you can't expect that bunch to ever find anything critical of the Soviets. Hell, they were shown victims and heard accounts of chemical attacks. Even got samples, but such things aren't 'significant' to the UN. Only the guys at *Soldier of Fortune* magazine seem to be telling the truth. They have current photographs of the *Voenno Khimicheskaya Voiska* using various chemical agents and in decontamination drill."

"Is that what worries you about this Roof of the Sky thing?"

"You're damn right it is. But even worse, what is the scope of this Soviet project? In Afghanistan, they are using chemical agents against noncombatants. In addition to the usual CN and CS agents, they have blister, blood and nerve gas in use. Then there's Yellow Rain, That's a series of toxic trichothecene substances made from a form of bread mold that has been endemic in Russia for a long time. It's not something you use against small concentrations of troops. Neither are Blue-X and the Flash. Yet there's evidence both have also been employed."

"Dan gave me a lot of this already," Mark responded.

"Okay. So what are their targets? Have you given that thought?"

"No. Not really."

"City areas, Mark. Maybe a lot of cities. And how are they going to deliver it covertly? Oh, there's so much about this we do not know. I want the answers to those questions even more than to simply break up their play before it gets rolling. If we don't know, we can't protect ourselves in the future. If, in fact, we have any chance of protecting the West from such hideous weapons." Sam rose from the table. "I've got to make a call. Back in a moment."

Twenty minutes later a man entered the restaurant and came to their table. The cut of his clothes and his hair style identified him as a Russian even more surely than his accent. The Penetrator tensed himself and slid one hand over the butt of the suppressed High Standard.

"It is good to see you, Samantha. How are you feeling?"

"A little light-headed at this altitude, Pyotr. This is my colleague, Steve Taylor," she introduced, using Mark's new cover name. "Pyotr Dvenynoy."

Pyotr took a seat. "I am afraid that my leaving and meeting you here has blown my cover. I was followed. And Yatsor is aware of your descriptions and involvement."

"We know that. For the past—how many years, Pyotr, twenty?—Pyotr has been a deep-cover agent for the Company inside the VKV, the chemical forces," Sam explained to Mark. "He managed to get word to his contact that he had been assigned to Krisha Mira, although at the time he had no idea what the project was about. Do you know anything more now?"

Dvenynoy accepted a glass of wine and sipped it. "Some. I do know that certain chemical agents, along with some biological weapons, have arrived in Bolivia. They are stored, or at least were stored, at a hidden depot in the Beni Department. What they consist of I do not know, and now never will. All *Voenno Khimicheskaya Voiska* personnel have been alerted to report to the supply dump within the next two days. I have been staying at the cultural mission compound. Now KGB knows I am an agent. My life is endangered by this, but I want to help in every way I can."

"Do you know for a certainty where the headquarters of Kirsha Mira is located?" Mark inquired.

"I am sorry, but no. That is a carefully kept secret."

"What about Tiahuanaco?"

"The City of the Dead?" Dvenynoy frowned. "I would tend to doubt that. That area is a national relic, am I correct? It would be something most difficult for even the KGB to arrange."

"We have information that indicates the site is somehow involved," the Penetrator persisted.

"Then you must verify this, no? Can I help?"

"Not right now. Go to ground, after you lose your tail," the Penetrator informed him. "Do you have a safe house to go to?"

"*Nyet*. But I do have arrangements made at a small hostel in the Miraflores district. It is on Avenida Petit Thouars, the Hostal Miraflores. The phone number is four-five-eight-seven-four-five."

Samantha placed her small hand on the back of his large, square one, covering the short, black bristles. "Be careful, Pyotr. Make sure you break their surveillance before you go to the hostel. And, *zhelahyou oodachee*."

"Good luck to you, too."

8

CITY OF THE DEAD

"Are you sure this is the only road to Tia-huanaco?" Sam asked when the Land Rover jounced into yet another huge pothole.

"It's the *best* road," the Penetrator responded cheerily.

"It seems so . . . empty out here. Nothing but scrub and tall grass for miles. A person would never believe we are at thirteen thousand feet."

Their speed had been reduced to a needle-jiggling seventeen miles per hour after leaving the short stretch of paved road. Each foot of the forty-two-mile journey seemed to contain at least one rut, chuckhole or protruding rock. Mark swiveled the wheel like a schooner captain in a North Atlantic squall while the vastness of the Altiplano slowly engulfed them in an aching silence. At last they arrived, an hour before the gates opened for the day.

Mark suggested they get coffee from a little stand across the road. Inside the lunch room next to the stand they found a file of stools at a short service bar and a half-dozen square

tables with metal folding chairs. The menu
consisted of a hand-lettered sign posted on
one wall. It listed few items, though the fare
sounded substantial.

"Buenas días, señor, señora. Que quiere?"

"Buenas días," the Penetrator returned. *"Café
con leche y pan dulce, por favor."*

The sturdy young counterman, an Aymará
Indian, deftly poured two cups of blended hot
milk and thick, aromatic coffee, brought them
to the counter, then returned with a large
metal tray heaped with sweet rolls. Mark made
selections for them with a pair of metal tongs.

"Me llamo Carlos," the proprietor introduced
himself. *"Ustedesson norteamericanos?"*

"Sí. I am called Esteban and this is Martha,"
the Penetrator returned, using their cover
names.

"It is a great pleasure. You have come to
see the ruins?" Carlos made a huge shrug and
laughed at himself. "Of course you have. What
else is there out in all of this empty space?"

"Yes, I have been fascinated by them for a
long time. Why is Tiahuanaco called the City
of the Dead?" Mark asked.

Carlos hunched his shoulders again. "There
are stories, Señor Esteban. I may even tell
you some of them. Did you know that the
Incas feared this place like nothing else? It is
they who gave it the name of the City of the
Dead. Aymará legend says that the city was
built by a race of giants who later displeased
the creator, the god Viracocha. He killed them
all for it."

"Then this is not an Inca city?" Sam inquired in somewhat less perfect Spanish than Mark's.

"Oh, no. The Incas still wandered about Lake Titicaca in reed boats and fought among themselves when Tiahuanaco reached its peak," Carlos returned.

"Were they conquered and absorbed by the Inca, then?" Mark inquired.

"The city had been long dead when the Inca rose to great power," Carlos replied. "All that remained were some buildings that have now crumbled to ruins and the language. The Aymará, my people, still speak a form of what is believed to be their tongue. Everything else about them is a mystery. It was to the Inca, too. That is why they were afraid of going there. And I think they were smart to keep away, for there are times when I am certain that Tiahuanaco is haunted."

Mark and Samantha exchanged glances. They finished their pastry and coffee and rose. "Thank you for the information, Carlos," the Penetrator told him. "We may be back for something at noon."

"I will be here, señor. It is a pleasure to talk to someone interested in our past."

A gray-haired man in the uniform of a museum guard for the Ministry of Education and Culture met them at the gate and they paid a small admission price to have the services of a guide.

Immediately Mark was struck by the Gate of the Sun.

"The structure, made of one piece of ande-site rock," their guide told them, "weighs ten tons. It depicts the god figure, Viracocha. With him are forty-eight attendants, who approach his central figure from all parts of the face. The gate stands seven feet high by eleven wide. You will note the bands that streak the god's cheeks, each with lines of circles that apparently represent tears. A collection of hu-man heads hangs from his belt and Viracocha carries a staff in each hand, the top ends of which are formed into the shape of condors heads. The Collas, an Aymará-speaking people, say that all these mighty stoneworks were created by a race of giants that predate the Inca and even the earlier inhabitants of Tia-huanaco. The legend has it that Viracocha became so wrathful at the giants that he de-stroyed them all. That is why the later resi-dents erected the Gate of the Sun to him, telling the story of Viracocha's anger. If you will come this way, we will examine the Kalasasaya, or 'standing stones' compound."

"Oh, Steve," Sam softly exclaimed to the Penetrator. "I feel it even more here."

"Feel what?"

"The utter aloneness this ruin generates. Listen to that wind whispering through the dry, yellow grass. I feel . . . sort of deserted, as though I had been brought here and left alone with all those ancient gods. There's a stillness I can't quite define that seems to hover over the air, hanging, waiting for some-thing to happen."

"The Russians? You aren't going psycic on me, are you, Sam?"

"N-no. It's just ... dramatic. The rolling plateau, the ruins, past cultures in the dust."

Their guide interrupted. "The Kalasasaya plaza, where we now stand, is four hundred and forty-two by four hundred and twenty-six feet. The wall surrounding it was made of carefully formed and fitted stones, without the use of mortar, broken into segments by the perpendicular stone shafts about twenty feet high. The structure could have been a reception hall in a large palace or an outdoor marketplace. We presently have no way of knowing." The young, dark-complected guard smiled and gestured to the left. "Off to this side is the sunken courtyard and the entrance to an underground temple. We will visit it in a moment. That is where the well-known Ponce monolith is located, named for the government archaeologist who found it. To the other direction is the Akapana pyramid. The top of it was hollowed out by the conquistador, Don Pedro de Vargas, who thought it was filled with gold. He found none. But a great deal of artifacts were lost. How much of value, both monetarily and to our culture, is not known."

A sudden chill coursed down the Penetrator's spine when he gazed at the distant temple atop the two-step pyramid. Was he catching Sam's touch of mysticism? he wondered. Then a more practical consideration took over. If anyone wanted to erect an antenna system, the pyramid would be an ideal place. His glance conveyed his ruminations to Sam, who nodded in agreement.

In forty-five minutes, they had made a complete circuit of the ruins, ending at the Tiahuanaco Museum exhibit, housed to one side of the Akapana pyramid. Their guide left them then with an invitation to spend all the time they wished and examine the ruins in detail, also to be sure to visit the museum.

"Now we go see all the places our guide didn't take us," Mark informed Samantha. "We'll begin at the underground temple."

The asthmatic wheeze of a forced-air circulating system came from one corner of Gregor Yatsor's office cubical. The KGB station chief lay aside a file folder and looked up at the white-smocked man before him. How he hated Germans! Especially these ex-Nazi scum. They had an arrogance that even thirty-eight years of Marxist indoctrination could not knock out of them. This scientist, this Dr. Siegfried Moller happened to be one of the worst. Why hadn't Moscow staffed the project entirely with reliable Russians? Oh, he knew the answer, he had to admit.

Always the cautious one, almost paranoid in his concern for security, Andropov himself had made the decision. This way, were anyone to be caught, the majority would be from other nations and blame would not fall on the Soviet Union. Still playing at spy and counterspy, Yatsor thought derisively. Then he brought himself up with a harsh mental reprimand. Better not let himself think that way often. It could lead to a slip, some public mention of his thoughts. That could bring the Gulag. He set a smile on his large, round face, and his deep-set, pig eyes were glittering.

"What is it, Dr. Moller?"

"Comrade Yatsor, Everything is in readiness in my department. All of the VKV personnel have been notified and most have arrived at the depot to take charge of the substances to be used in the actual attack. All except Comrades Protopkin, Zukaric and Dvenynoy."

Mention of Pyotr Dvenynoy brought a rush of hot anger to Yatsor's face. The KGB major tried to keep his expression neutral while he thought of the defector. No! Worse than that, an agent in place with the deepest of deep cover. All these years. All the effort to train the man.

When the report had come to him from his underlings that Pyotr Dvenynoy had been followed to a restaurant where he had met with the American agents and later had evaded surveillance and made good his escape, Major Yatsor had exploded with rage. He carefully examined the two agents who had been assigned when Dvenynoy had made his unauthorized departure from the cultural mission. Had he not been checked out? He was supposed to have come from a small village outside Smolensk. His accent indicated he had. How then could he be an American agent planted in the ranks of the *Voenno Khimi cheskaya Voiska*? Dvenynoy's selection, fortu nately, had not been his doing, Yatsor reminded himself.

"Dvenynoy will not be going," he snapped at Moller, enjoying the surprised discomfort on the scientist's face. "It appears that some of your superiors in VKV made a serious error. Pyotr Ulanovich Dvenynoy was not what he seemed to be. He was not even a Soviet citizen. In fact, he is an American agent, planted on us by the CIA. When the actual substitution was made, we will probably never know. The fact remains, Herr Doktor, that Pyotr Ulanovich was, as our British associates would put it, 'a mole.' "

A rap on the doorframe brought Major Yatsor's attention beyond his visitor's shoulder to a plainclothes KGB guard standing there. "Yes?"

"Comrade Major, one of our aboveground lookouts has just reported that the American agents, the man and woman, are prowling around the streets of Tiahuanaco."

"What!" Yatsor clapped both hands together. "Well, it seems they have delivered themselves for the slaughter. Dr. Moller, you can forget about the treason of Lieutenant Dvenynoy. He will not dare show up at the depot now and his colleagues have apparently handed themselves up to us without any idea of what exists beneath their feet." He returned his attention to the guard. "Send Luis Torreos in."

When the Bolivian Communist leader arrived, Yatsor issued terse orders. "Comrade Torreos, take six men and go up on the streets above us. The American agents are here." At Torreos' startled expression, he went on triumphantly. "Yes. They have come to us, whether by accident or in an attempt to deepen their cover as tourists I don't know. All the same, we have them in our hands. Use silent methods, but one way or another, I want them both dead before the end of this day."

9

SLINGS OF
OUTRAGEOUS FORTUNE

The tall stone stela stood a few inches short of seven feet high. Its features, carved in relief, gazed at the Gate of the Sun, from its position in the sunken courtyard. The representation—whether god or man no one knew—appeared to be bearded and it made a gesture of either awe or warning. The right hand, palm out, rested over the heart, while the left crossed the abdomen, palm inward, little finger touching the navel. On its "kilt" a bas-relief pair of jaguars faced each other and stared outward. At the object's left rear two smaller pillars shared a joined-together platform of perfect squares that met at an upper and lower corner. On the foremost one, animal heads had been carved into the stone and looked in all four directions.

"He seems to be trying to tell us something," Samantha Chase observed in a hushed tone.

"Yeah. That we're on a fool's errand. We've been over this fifty acres twice now and haven't seen any mysterious, unexplained structures or a single Russian," Mark told her.

"But you said that Hovey . . ."

"True enough. He also had a badly infected wound. He could have been brought out here for interrogation, or have visited the place in an attempt to establish his cover and then hallucinated the whole thing when his condition deteriorated."

Their footsteps crunched on the neatly raked gravel floor of the sunken courtyard as they started away in the opposite direction, headed for the Akapana pyramid. They had taken a dozen steps when a rough-edged stone whirred past Sam's head and cracked noisily against the fitted rock wall. Instinctively she and the Penetrator dropped to the ground.

"Who's throwing rocks at us?" Sam asked, her voice edged with agitation.

"From the force, I'd say whoever it was used a sling," Mark observed. Another missile whipped by overhead. "We're too exposed. We have to make a run for it. Try to spot the slinger."

When gravel gouted up a foot from Mark's head, they both rose and dashed toward the shelter of a trio of pillars. A fourth projectile zipped between them and clattered off the wall. Another ten feet and they reached cover.

"Over there," Sam announced while she pointed behind her.

The Penetrator drew his silenced High Standard. A quick look around showed him the cleverness of the unknown attackers. They had been effectively cut off from the only way out of the sunken courtyard. He saw a blur of movement and the slinger exposed himself for a brief instant, arm over his head, the Inca-style sling whirling around in a great arc. Mark took quick, though careful, aim.

A poison-filled .22-caliber hollowpoint tore into the slinger's left shoulder joint. He dropped his weapon and staggered out of sight, his mouth puckered into a moan of pain. Immediately three more small rocks splintered into shards against the stone column near the Penetrator's face. One struck him above the left eye and a thin trickle of blood began to run down his face.

"The staircase. We've got to make it over there or we'll be trapped down here. When I take a shot at one of those other men, make a run for it."

Another slinger stepped into the open to launch his missile and caught a deadly .22 slug in the sternum. He arched backward, turned and tried to run, but already the poison had begun to take effect. He sagged on weary legs and shuffled only three steps toward cover before he fell. His legs convulsed in a moribund tattoo and then he spread out in the ultimate relaxation of death.

Sam had two yards to cover to the foot of the stairs leading up out of the courtyard. Suddenly she lurched sideways and let out a little yelp of pain.

"What's going on out there?" A cultural ministry guard stood at the head of the steps, hand on the butt of the Argentine Ballester Molina .45 in his holster.

A POR guerrilla stepped into view and released his stone. It struck the guard in the temple with enough force to snap his head to the opposite side. He swayed for a moment, then tumbled partway down the staircase to lie in a crumpled heap. Blood trickled from his ears and nose. The Penetrator acted immediately.

Two bullets sped from the High Standard. The first took the guard's killer in the throat. Reflexively he grabbed at the injured area, his eyes bugged out and his mouth worked, though no sound came. His knees buckled as the poison took hold and he fell face-first to the gravel paving.

The second round plowed into the low forehead of the assassin who had hit Sam on the outside of her left thigh. His arm jerked downward and the sling twined around his mouth and throat. His feet moved without direction, forcing him a step forward before he dropped without a sound.

"You okay?" the Penetrator asked his companion.

"Sure. Only sore as hell."

"Then run. Get up the stairs."

"Where will you be?"

"Right behind you. Go!"

Sling stones rattled around them while Samantha limped in the lead. The Penetrator paused once, long enough to throw a shot at their assailants, which missed. The small slug smeared lead on the gravel flooring and whined off across the vast Altiplano. Together they dodged around the body of the dead guard and gained the top. Quickly they slipped in among some fallen blocks of andesite.

"There's still some of them out there, Sam. Try to work your way to the main gate."

"What if they have men covering there?"

"We'll play hell trying to take them out without being spotted. We worry about that one when we get there."

Sam moved away, feeling a chill of apprehension that the thin sun of the Andes could not dispel. Behind her, the Penetrator began a deadly game of hide and seek.

"They got away, Comrade Torreos," one POR gunman complained. He tucked his sling in his belt and drew a Red Chinese Type 51 pistol.

"Not that," Luis Torreos ordered gruffly. "We are supposed to do this quietly. It's bad enough that Ortiz killed the guard. The government is bound to look into that."

"The American agent killed Ortiz, so what is to worry?"

"And we have to recover his body. In fact, that is a good job for you, comrade."

A shrill whistle sounded from above. One of Torreos' men appeared at the edge of the sunken courtyard and waved his arm in a signal that indicated the Americans had been found.

"We can save that for later. Come on."

Quickly Torreos gathered his men and issued terse orders. "Contreras, you and Ojeda cover the gate. Don't let them out. Urubio,

Portrero, Gonzales, go to the left, circle around. You two, come with me."

Torreos drew his knife, a long, thin-bladed stiletto, and led his men out in a circular pattern to the right. Everywhere tourists hampered their search. At last, Torreos caught a flicker of furtive movement to his left and he swung that way, his arm rising to a spot beside his right ear.

Then he saw the big-shouldered form of the American and let the knife fly through the air.

The Penetrator spun at the matallic ringing when Torreos' blade caromed off a stone pillar six inches behind his back. Mark brought up his High Standard only to find he had no target. He hurried on, seeking his enemy while he worked steadily toward the main entrance. Suddenly two squat Bolivians appeared in front of him.

One carried a machete and the other a suppressed Makarov. The Penetrator shot the gunman first.

The sizzling .22 slug struck him in the left nipple, and even though the poison burst directly into his heart, he had time to raise the Soviet 9mm pistol and take a shot at the Penetrator.

With an air-splitting crack, the bullet snapped past the Penetrator's head, so close that its heat could be felt on his earlobe. Reflexively he jerked to one side and sent another lead pellet toward the POR guerrilla.

It gave Rafael Ojeda a third nostril, centered in the curving hawk beak of his nose. His head snapped back like a boxer taking a short, sharp jab and he keeled over like a stalk of wilted celery. Instantly his partner, Contreras, leaped forward swinging his machete.

Mark fired a shot that missed, then had to block the descending steel with the suppressor tube that surrounded the barrel of his High Standard. Sparks flew and a rent appeared in the metal. The Penetrator cursed his luck. He had replaced the one damaged by a bullet and had only one more left. In a flash his other hand came up, fingers closing over the pocket clip trigger of his Guardfather.

The long, spring-loaded spike slithered out, locked into place with a soft click and the Penetrator felt a solid jar in the palm of his hand when the needle point rammed into the hard roof of Contreras' mouth, skidded off and plunged through his soft palate and deep into his brain.

Contreras blinked rapidly and two tears formed in his eyes a fraction of a second before they glazed over and he went slack, sagging into the Penetrator's arms.

Mark lowered him to the ground, removed the Guardfather and wiped it clean on Contreras' baggy alpaca sweater. For purposes of a momentary disguise, the Penetrator donned the dead man's poncho and chullo, the ubiquitous wollen hat of Bolivia. Silently he started off once more.

"Over here!" a voice called in Spanish. "The girl is trying for the gate!"

Mark glanced up and to his right and saw Sam making a concentrated dash for the entrance way. Her legs churned and she high-stepped it like a championship class 440 runner. A slinger stepped into the open and began to swing his deadly weapon. The Penetrator brought up his High Standard and took steady aim. He gently squeezed the finely tuned trigger.

His shot struck home, but not before Juan Urubio released a small stone. It proved to be his last conscious act in life and he didn't even get to see it strike Sam in the back of her head. She dropped like a felled deer, only a split second before her attacker went down with a poisoned bullet in his brain.

Mark holstered his High Standard and sprinted to where Sam lay. The damaged suppressor had allowed a louder pop than normally expected, though it seemed not to have attracted any undue attention. He reached Sam's side and knelt, his face drawn with anxiety and oblivious to any further danger. He doubted there would be any. The incident had drawn a small crowd of tourists and government workers.

"Sam! Are you all right, Sam?"

Samantha groaned and relapsed into loose-boned unconsciousness. Mark examined the area of the wound and his hand came away sticky with a thin smear of blood. Gently he rolled Sam onto her back and peeled open an eyelid. The pupil seemed normal to him. He checked the other and found it the same—neither dilated nor contracted.

"What is it? What happened, señor?"

"Someone attacked her. A mugger, I think."

"*Que?* What is a 'mugger'?"

"A thief. *Un ladrón.*"

"*Ay, sí! Yo lo creo.* But why here?"

Mark ignored the question. "Help me carry her over there." He nodded toward Carlos's lunch stand. "I need some water to revive her and a place where she can recover."

The young archaeologist who had been questioning Mark squatted down and assisted the Penetrator in picking up Sam. Together they walked over to a low bench to one side of the small lunchroom attached to Carlos's stand. The proprietor came running over, wringing his hands on a spotted apron.

"What happened?"

"Someone hit her, Carlos."

"*Ay de mí!* I will call the police."

"No. That won't be necessary," the Penetrator urged.

"Since this terrible thing happened on government property, señor, I shall attend to the *policia*. It is necessary, you understand?" the archaeologist remarked, concern darkening his sun-leathered face.

"Really, it is not important."

"I insist," the implacable scientist countered.

Mark shrugged. "Get me some water, Carlos. And a bottle of *agua mineral* for her to drink."

"*En seguida, señor!*" He turned away, making shooing motions at the curious spectators who had crowded his establishment. "The rest of you back up! Clear out of here and give us room to help the poor lady. Go on, go on."

They straggled out slowly, reluctantly, and Carlos returned in a minute with a folded square of wet cloth and a small bottle of bubbling water. Mark wiped Sam's dust-smeared face and then lightly dabbed at the area where the stone had struck her. Sam had regained shaky consciousness by the time the young government archaeologist returned with two policemen in tow.

"Now, what is this about being attacked?" the senior of the officers inquired. He pushed the blue-and-tan garrison cap back from his forehead and hooked both thumbs behind the wide gun leather that circled his spreading middle.

"We were on our way over here for some lunch when suddenly a man leaped at Martha there and struck her. I think he wanted to steal her purse."

"That is most unusual," the cop observed. "We have little crime out here. Nothing light enough to steal." He chuckled at his own poor joke.

"But it is the truth, I tell you," Mark protested.

"Hummm. Perhaps. But there is the matter of some men we have found among the ruins. Men who have been shot to death. Do you, by any chance, carry a pistol?"

"No. Of course not. I abhor those dangerous things. Besides, isn't it illegal for a foreign national to have a firearm in Bolivia?"

"Under most circumstances, yes. I was . . . only curious."

"Tell us again how this happened?" the younger policeman inserted.

Before Mark could begin, Carlos spoke to him in sotto voce. *"Tu empeñes en hacerte el italiano*. I will take care of this." He turned to the police officers, spread his hands wide in a placating gesture. "The gentleman is telling the truth. I, myself, saw it. He and the Señora Martha were walking here when someone attacked them. A tall man, dark complexion, maybe a Quechua. He ran when Señor Esteban swung a fist at him."

"You know these people, then, Carlos?" the fat cop asked.

"Of a certainty I do. They are old friends."

"Very well. We will accept their story. It is most irregular, though. But we do have a lot of work, reports to file, long hours of overtime regarding the dead men. Are you sure, señor, that you know nothing about that?"

Mark made a helpless gesture. "Nothing at all. I am sorry I can't help you."

The police left and the Penetrator turned to Carlos. "It was nice of you to support us like that. But why did you?"

Carlos shrugged. A sly glint flickered in his eyes. "I saw part of what happened. I also saw what you did to those last two men. For that I am thankful, for I have observed those faces before. They are bad, evil men. I have long believed that they are foreign grave robbers, ladrones who are looting my nation's history and heritage. Now, I think there is more involved, no?"

"There might be." The Penetrator shrugged it off.

"I mentioned before that I believe the ruins to be haunted. The reason is that on many nights I hear sounds come from there. Noises that should not be."

The Penetrator's eyes widened and he shot a cautionary glance at Sam. "Can you tell us more about these sounds?"

"If you are doing what I think you are, it would be my pleasure." He paused and, at Mark's nod, went on. "At first it was like men digging. Yet each morning, nothing had been unearthed nor were there signs of anything being removed. Later it was voices and once or twice the sound of an automobile, though I never saw one. Only two nights ago, I heard a high-pitched squeal, like the cries of a very small *puerco*."

"Could it have been a radio?" the Penetrator prompted.

Carlos frowned, lacking a solid reference point. "I have not had much experience with a radio, Esteban. For all I know it could have been the grandfather of all radios and I would not recognize it. It was loud, though. It wailed up and down and lasted for more than two minutes."

Again a significant glance passed between Mark and Sam. "How do you feel?" the Penetrator asked her.

"Much better. I . . . I think I can move around now."

"Then we should be going." He rose and turned to Carlos. "Thank you for all your help,

Carlos. Maybe the sounds you heard have something to do with the men who attacked us. Perhaps not. We will let you know. Thanks again."

Once back in the Land Rover, well away from Tiahuanaco, the Penetrator let a wide, relaxed smile of victory spread on his face. "I think we have found our connection."

10

INTERNATIONAL EFFORT

Pain still flared from a large purple, green and yellow bruise on the outside of Samantha Chase's left thigh. Its throbbing blended with waves of torment that radiated from the tennis-ball-sized lump at the back of her head. She sat, somewhat gingerly, on a chair in the Penetrator's room at the Gloria, an hour after their return to town. She sipped from a glass of *pisco* and ice while Mark paced the floor, his mind combing over the events of their day.

"This isn't the best painkiller," Sam observed. "But it beats hell out of codeine."

"Which is all I had in my medical kit. Sorry, kid."

"No need to be. It's me who got her big head in the way. What have we really got? I was a bit woozy when you were talking with Carlos."

"From what he said, I think we can be sure now that somehow the Soviets have managed to set up their operation for Krisha Mira at Tiahuanaco. Where, exactly, is another question. I think . . ."

A knock on the door interrupted the Penetrator's interpretation of Carlos's revelations. He frowned briefly and walked across the room to open it.

"Yes?"

"You are Señor Esteban Fletcher?"

The visitor had to look up from his five-foot nine-inch height to address the Penetrator. Bright, black eyes glittered with intelligence in an open, friendly face. At Mark's assurance that he had the right room, the man went on.

"I am Mario Campos. May I come in?"

"What is it you want, Señor Campos?" the Penetrator demanded, not relinquishing his place in the doorway.

Campos raised a cautionary hand. "Please. It is better if we discuss it inside. I am sure you understand." He spoke his last words with a conspiratorial tone.

The Penetrator stepped aside and let Campos enter, closed the door behind him, then slapped the man against it and gave him a quick frisk. Mark removed an Argentine Ballester Molina .45 automatic from a shoulder holster. He held it by finger and thumb in front of the visitor.

"Perhaps you can explain this, Señor Campos?"

Campos shrugged, his hands making small, palms-up gestures near his shoulders. "Certainly. I am Captain Mario Campos, of the intelligence service of the Bolivian army. I have come to discuss with you what you have learned about Project Krisha Mira."

It took some effort, yet the Penetrator was

able to control his surprise and turned a blank face to Captain Campos. "I don't know what that is, Captain. Could you be a bit more specific?"

"Come now, Señor Fletcher. The Bolivian government is quite aware of increased Soviet activities within our borders. Also of the intervention of American agents of the CIA and other intelligence organizations. Krisha Mira is the latest Soviet effort toward conquest of the Western Hemisphere. It is a multifaceted operation, involving small, secret bases here and in neighboring countries. What we don't know, and believe that you do, is the purpose and function of these bases."

Tension built in the room. Sam had slipped her hand into her purse, her fingers curled around the grip of a silenced .380 AMT Backup. Mark had fisted Campos's Ballester Molina and pointed the muzzle at the Bolivian officer. The Penetrator's eyes had narrowed and his mouth hardened to a thin, grim line.

"When we were contacted about Kirsha Mira by your National Security Council, we were advised that I should use the term 'intercept' and it might have some meaning to you," Campos went on.

The Penetrator relaxed slightly at use of the mission code name. "Go on."

"Washington is getting concerned. Time goes by and yet you have not made a report. Also, more Soviet operatives, using the usual diplomatic covers, have entered Bolivia in the past three days. That causes us worry. So then, what, if anything, have you discovered?"

"I think we know where the central core of Krisha Mira is located."

"Ah, excellent! Where might that be, Señor Fletcher?"

"If we're going to work together, call me Steve. The Soviets appear to have managed to install some sort of transmitter and an antenna system at Tiahuanaco."

"B-but . . . that is patently impossible," Campos exploded. "The ruins are under the strictest government supervision."

"And only . . ." The Penetrator glanced at his Rolex Oyster. "Two and a half hours ago, one of the government guards out there was killed by a stone, hurled by what appeared to be an Inca sling. The purpose of that attack was to kill, uh, Martha and me. She received a hit in one thigh and a wound on the back of her head. From the appearance of the killers, and from past experience, I would say they were from the *Partido Obrero Revolucionario*."

"When you speak of past experience, Steve, would that include the bodies at El Alto and the Plaza Hotel?"

"In the past few days I have managed to make 'good Communists' out of a number of POR members," the Penetrator evaded.

"I . . . see. Well, then, I think we can do business. We understand each other's trade craft. What happened at Tiahuanaco?" Campos concluded.

Quickly Mark filled him in, ending his recitation with a grisly, accurate summation. "I terminated as many as I could."

"Coupled with what your agent had in his

last report"—Campos carefully avoided any mention of Hovey's name or his death—"I would say that your theory regarding the Soviet main base has to be correct, no matter how bizarre and impossible it seems."

"Thank you, Captain."

"If I am to call you Steve, you should make that Mario."

"Good enough, Mario." The Penetrator seemed to discover for the first time that he still held Captain Campos's pistol. "Uh, here. I think you should have this back."

Mario took it and returned the .45 to his shoulder holster. "What do you plan now?"

"We were just discussing that when you arrived. Before anything can be done, we have to *find* what we are looking for," the Penetrator began, expressing the obvious. "Another daylight soft probe is out. I propose that we visit Tiahuanaco at night, when we have a bit more freedom of movement."

"When did you have in mind?"

"Tonight, Mario."

"Won't the Soviets, if they are indeed somewhere in the ruins, have increased security after today's incident?"

"Certainly. I'm sure, though, that you are familiar with how men behave on night watch. So far, the Soviets seem to be using POR members for their security screen. They are primarily guerrillas, right? That means that no matter how much their training, they are not the highly disciplined troops one could find in the Bolivian army or were they Soviet regulars. We will wait until lethargy and boredom begin to set in during the last hours of the final guard trick. With dark clothing and blackened faces, we should be able to move around with relative safety."

"Good. When we find whatever the Soviets are doing, what comes next? A worldwide exposé? A formal protest to the United Nations?"

"Are you kidding?" the Penetrator asked derisively. "Our assignment is to destroy everything."

"By that you mean equipment, vehicles, that sort of thing?"

"By that I mean *everything*," the Penetrator returned coolly.

"Let me understand this clearly. Precisely what is your part of this operation, Steve?"

"I am to terminate every Russian son of a bitch involved in Krisha Mira."

Silence held in the small room and a deadly aura seemed to emanate from the Penetrator's rugged, hawk-nosed, high cheekboned features.

Not the slightest bit of static distorted the clarity of voice over the satellite-directed radio net. Major Gregor Yatsor sat at his desk and conversed with the deputy minister of defense of the Soviet Union, Marshal Dmitri F. Ustinov.

"Yes, Comrade Minister. Let me express the gratitude that both Dr. Moller and I feel for the manner in which you have organized *Krisha Mira* and the cooperation you have achieved between the Politbureau and the *Voenno Khimicheskaya Voiska* commanders.

Everything has arrived precisely on schedule. We have sufficient men and materials to carry out our mission and a few to spare."

"I am concerned by these reports you have sent me regarding intervention by the Americans and the activities of their agents. What is the present status of that situation?"

"As my reports indicate, one has been eliminated. The other two have been identified, which is the same as to say they have been neutralized. So far they have no idea where the operations base is for the project. I do wish that I did not have to work with our Bolivian comrades."

"How is that?"

"They are so unspeakably incompetent. As you know, they missed two opportunities to eliminate the Americans. That cost me a good man. Then, this morning, the Americans came to the ruins. They were identified immediately and I dispatched Comrade Torreos and some of his men to deal with it. They drove the Americans off and wounded the woman. But again they failed to finish off a mere two people."

"Won't that draw the American's suspicions to the true location of your control center?"

"Not necessarily, Comrade Minister. Attempts were made in differing places before. Their natural assumption would be that this was only one more. Besides, even if they concentrated their efforts on the ruins, by the time they found how to get into the installation, it would be too late."

A surprised gasp came over the micro-beam. "You mean you are that close?"

"Yes, Comrade Minister. It is only a matter of days . . . hours actually, before the test run can be made with an empty missile. After that, within three days we can activate the project."

"Marvelous, Gregor. You know that Krisha Mira is an extremely sensitive and highly important undertaking. If I had not known you since you were a boy, and been positive of your loyalty and industry, I would never have accepted you for the post. Of course, the premier had nothing but good to say about you. Now, about the rockets you will use. You are satisfied that they will perform as anticipated?"

"Yes," Yatsor replied, a dubious quality in his voice. "This old Viktor-Oden model has sufficient range. The Germans proved that with their early type used on England. We encountered problems, though, in installing the new guidance equipment. Of course the payload is not so large with Agent *Pakaznoy* or *Khah-cen'yeye*. Still, I would have prefered SS twenty-twos for the *Zholtenaya Dozh't*. For all of them, in fact."

"The logistics of moving such large units in secrecy prevented that, as you know. Even if the components could have been assembled there, the time factor made it impossible. Never worry, Gregor, with such powerful weapons as Agent Flash, Blue-X and Yellow Rain," the deputy minister went on, naming the chemical and biological agents in the same order as Yatsor, "you will have no difficulty at all." Abruptly, he changed the subject. "Then the next time I hear from you will be?"

"When the test flight is complete."

"I had hoped it would be when the Americans are eliminated."

"I shall do my utmost toward that goal, Comrade Minister."

A heavy sigh gusted from Gregor Yatsor's thick lips when the conversation ended. He picked up the long wooden needles and set them to clicking while he ran another line of the alpaca yarn. Three days ago he had started another sweater, made in the traditional styles and colors of the Aymará Indians. It was a hobby he had picked up to soothe his strained mental processes and to escape from the pressures of his command position. This one would be for little Gregor Gregorivich, just turned thirteen and ready to enter the special service school provided for children of KGB personnel.

This thought brought another sigh from Major Yatsor. How he missed his family. Since he had earned a supervisory desk job in Moscow eleven years before, this had been his first field assignment. Unlike many of his contemporaries, he had been afforded the luxury of watching his children grow. He had to admit he loved his namesake most of all.

A sturdy, happy child, Gregor Gregorivich had the stocky body of a peasant and the quick mind of a Lenin. He would go far in the Soviet hierarchy. Especially with the patronage of his father. The elder Yatsor had been promised direct promotion to the rank of colonel for the successful completion of Krisha

Mira and command of an entire KGB section. With his guidance, and the friendly support of Ustinov and Premier Andropov, little Gregor Gregorivich would achieve great things. The thought made Major Gregor Yatsor happy . . . nearly as contented as contemplation of the deaths of the American agents.

11

NIGHT VISITORS

An early moon had long since set when the Penetrator started the Land Rover to drive the last five miles of their journey to Tiahuanaco. He had driven thirty of the forty-three miles by the light of the heavens and would stop a kilometer short of their goal for the final walk-in. Mario Campos sat next to Mark, navigating by use of an infrared night scope he had obtained from the army. Sam sat in the back with the rest of their hastily gathered equipment.

"Slow down and steer left," Mario announced. "There's a rut in line with the right wheel."

"This is worse than being talked down to the runway in zero visibility," the Penetrator observed.

"There aren't any chuckholes in the sky," Mario returned.

"You're a pilot?" Mark inquired.

"I have my first class," Mario returned proudly. "That is the same as a private license in your country."

"When this is all over, we'll have to take a little run around the Andes."

"I'd like that," Mario returned sincerely.

"Count me out," Sam groaned from behind them. "Flying around mountains gives me the willies. And at this altitude . . . I want a pressurized cabin."

"You're going soft in your old age, Martha," the Penetrator kidded.

"Not far now," Mario observed. "Over that rise we can park the Rover and start walking."

Mark divided his attention between the Stygian night and invisible road and last-minute instructions. "We'll want to shoot bearings on all the prominent structures and sketch a rough map. That way if we do find some sort of underground complex we will be able to orient ourselves with the ground above."

"How do we do that without being spotted?" Sam inquired.

The Penetrator patted his breast pocket. "I have a little gadget right here to take care of that problem." Some time back, he went on to explain, he had seen an article in *Soldier of Fortune* Magazine about an improvised map light that used a penlight barrel, a resistor and a red light-emitting diode.

"So I made up a few of them. They do come in handy," he concluded. "The nice part is that even with the cost of a penlight, they only run around three dollars to make."

Mario had been sweeping the countryside with his scope. He put it down and turned to Mark. "There's a good spot over on the right. A little ridge will cut off view from the road in case someone comes along."

"Okay, lead the way."

When the Land Rover came to a stop, the three persons climbed out and shouldered light nylon packs. The Penetrator reached back inside for his Sidewinder. Mario eyed it with trepidation. Even with the fat tube of the McQueen suppressor it represented a special danger he wished to avoid.

"I don't know about that," he remarked. "The government would have a screaming fit if we bullet-scarred any of the antiquities at the ruins."

"Underground it won't matter, right? So it goes along," the Penetrator advanced with finality.

In their dark clothing, faces and hands smeared with black, military grease paint, Mark, Sam and Mario blended with the night. They moved smoothly, cautiously, avoiding any betraying crunch of gravel or crackle of dry, yellow grass. It took the better part of an hour to cover the last kilometer to the fence around Tiahuanaco.

The Penetrator peered at his watch. "Zero-three-twenty. We couldn't have timed it better. We'll go in when this batch of sentries are at their lowest ebb and time our exfiltration for when their replacements are in the same condition."

"Providing they follow a standard military-watch schedule," Mario reminded him.

"With the Russians running things, you can

be sure of that," Mark whispered to him. "Okay, here we go."

Mark attached one of several sets of bypass jumpers to the fence to keep the alarm system operative. He used a thick jacket to muffle the sound of a set of heavy wire cutters while he snipped their way through the fabric of the cyclone fence. When finished, he peeled back a triangular flap and urged the other two ahead.

Sam entered first. She bellied her way to one side and trained her suppressed AMT .380 on the expanse to their front.

Mario came next and took the opposite side, the fat bulk of a MAC suppressor attached to the snout of the extension barrel in his Ballester Molina. The Penetrator followed, on his back, and closed the gap. Like the trained professionals they were, they waited a full ten minutes before moving forward. So far they had seen no indication of any guards.

But, yeah, they were there all right.

The Penetrator spotted the first one and motioned his companions to spread out and go around.

Hushed, in a cloak of blackness, they negotiated the first line of sentries and reached the mortarless stone wall. The Penetrator tapped each companion on one shoulder, then whispered in their ears.

"We split up here. Each take a section and look for anything out of the ordinary. Make note of everything, no matter how insignificant it may seem. And be quiet. We'll meet at the Gate of the Sun."

Each searcher faded into the darkness, intent on the sector to be searched. The Penetrator went up and over the seven-foot wall and dropped noiselessly to the other side. He skirted the fallen blocks and leaning spires, working his way in among the ruins where he and Sam had their final encounter with the POR gunmen. Nothing could be so perfectly hidden that no trace of its existence could be found. His eyes and hands probed the ground around him.

Suddenly an undulating layer of warm, moist air brushed his cheek. He caught the scent of perspiration and human body odor. Mark expanded his finely tuned senses, seeking what he knew must be nearby. He cast to right and left and slowly advanced, bent double. Then he had it!

Cleverly built into the crack in a split stone of monumental proportions, he found what had to be an air shaft. Thin tendrils of mist, caused by the chill of the Altiplano air reacting to the warmer, wet draft rising from the narrow well, floated close to the opening. It wouldn't be coming from directly below, he reasoned, so where?

Quickly he shot bearings on the Akapana pyramid and, in the opposite direction, the Gate of the Sun. He divided the angle by ninety degrees and sighted along the black hairlines in the arms of his lensatic compass. The Kalasasaya plaza.

Yes, it fit. Confidently the Penetrator worked his way from shadow to shadow until he stood in the center of the great paved square. If I were a Russian, where would I put a secret entrance? Mark pondered, using the "boy and the horse" method. He turned slowly, keeping low to the ground. Unless they had constructed it in the form of a perfect airlock, it should be emitting telltale vapors in the night air. He moved to one side and began a detailed search.

Nothing.

Along the second side, he found the same. With growing doubt, he started along the third leg.

A rooting-hog snort alerted the Penetrator that his idea hadn't been so bad after all. He crept forward, found a snoring guard, a short, stocky Bolivian and scooted down between two blocks of stone. A few feet beyond him, ghostly in the pale starlight, he saw three wavering tendrils of vapor. Mark eased himself forward and examined the disguised entrance to the mystery they had come to unravel. Satisfied, he left the guard unmolested and made his way to the Gate of the Sun.

Ten precious minutes passed before Sam glided in out of the obsidian night. Mark signaled her to wait quietly. He leaned back against the inner arch of the doorway in the gate and bided his time until Mario arrived.

"I've found it," he whispered tersely. "On the west wall of the Kalasasaya plaza. We have to get in position, wait until the guard changes and then take out the new one."

At five minutes after four, the watch was relieved. The new sentry paced about, fresh and alert. For five minutes more, the Penetrator timed his movements, then struck.

A soft nylon garrot settled soundlessly over the guard's head. Before the startled man could react, the thin mesh strip crossed behind his back and bit into the flesh of his neck. The Penetrator gave it a powerful jerk and twist, then pivoted under his arms and hoisted the man off his feet.

The dying man kicked and writhed to no avail, a thin hissing sound emerging from his gaping mouth. Blood pounded at his temples and a red haze obscured the star-spattered velvet sky. Slowly his struggles ceased and his body went limp. Urine wet the front of his trousers and a fetid stench rose when he voided his bowels. Mark eased him to the ground and motioned his companions forward.

It took the Penetrator less than a minute to figure out the concealed latch system and open the pivoting stone block. Cautiously he entered, Sam and Mario at his back.

"Kto eto?" a voice called in Russian from ahead.

"Eto Boris, Tovarish," the Penetrator replied.

When the KGB guard showed himself in the dim red light of the tunnel, the Penetrator blasted him off to that Big Comintern in the Sky with a three-round burst from the silenced Sidewinder.

"Let's get moving," he ordered, dragging the dead guard out of sight.

"What do you think, sister-wife?" a male, tenor voice purred while two unseen observers watched the Penetrator and his small force disappear underground.

"By all means, we must have the girl. She will be perfect for the moon rites, my brother-husband." Her small mouth twisted into a smile and she brushed her lips lightly with the tip of her tongue. Despite the cold night air, she wore only a wraparound skirt of tightly woven alpaca fleece worked through with the mystic symbols of the ancient Aymará Cult of the Moon Goddess and a heavy gorget of gold, inlaid with onyx and amethyst. The latter barely covered her pertly upstanding, youthful breasts.

Huascar Capac smiled mirthlessly. The well-formed muscles of his broad shoulders and naked chest rippled when he folded his arms across his body and gazed downward slightly at his younger sister. His full lips turned down scornfully and a light of disdain flickered in his close-set eyes that smoldered above the hawk bridge of his nose.

"What about the men?" he asked her.

The woman, who called herself Yahuar Ocllo, shrugged indifferently. "You can have them. Viracocha needs propitiating also. They are of no importance to me."

"A divine priestess who scorns such worthy sacrifices? Their skills nearly match those of Aymará warriors of old. What will our followers say?"

"They will be grateful for what we give them, as will the gods. It has been too long, far too long, since the proper rites have been offered up. Tell me, my brother-husband, when will Veracocha return and drive the poisonous foreigners from our land?"

Although short of stature, standing only five feet six inches, Huascar Capac had to look down at his little sister, who had also become his wife, in the tradition of the Inca and pre-Inca rulers. Since childhood they had been taught the secrets and coached in the roles they were to fulfill as adults: High Priest of the Sun and Priestess of the Moon, he thought. Although cynicism sometimes threatened to overwhelm him, and his faith in what they had been told to believe wavered, Yahuar—once named Teresa as he had once been called Raul—remained steadfast. She had an almost childlike quality of assurance, he reflected, that Veracocha was real and that he would actually return, to manifest himself in visible form and destroy those who had defiled their sacred homeland.

His contemplation softened his cynical heart and erased his scorn. "Soon. Very soon now, beloved sister."

Yahuar looked up appealingly at her elder brother, a light of reverence and passion swimming in her wide-set eyes. Her smooth features, usually delightfully arranged in a youthful visage of innocent trust and love, twisted now, and hot, angry words came from behind her small, even white teeth.

"And what of the evil ones who desecrate our sacred ruins by dwelling beneath them?"

"They shall be the last to perish. For them is reserved a slow death, most painful and frightening to contemplate."

"Though in our lifetime, Huascar, is that not so?"

"Truly, my dear little Yahuar."

Their parents had given them the names of the first man and first woman, created by

Veracocha in the Time of Mists, when they had wed in a secret ceremony, far out on the Altiplano. Yahuar truly believed herself the reincarnation of a demigoddess and Huascar often believed himself to be the son of a powerful god—particularly when he had been seized by the compelling madness of the hypnotic rites of his sun cult.

Suddenly Yahuar rose on tiptoe and embraced her brother, her slender arms exerting surprising strength in the short display of affection. He felt a stirring in his loins at the warm pressure of her slender, gracefully formed body. They both sighed with inner contentment, then her capricious mind abruptly took a new course.

"I was but ten years grown when our wise parents supervised our first mating, brother mine. We were to be the leaders, they decreed, the high priest and priestess of the sun and moon." Huascar experienced a momentary jolt of surprise and superstitious awe when his sister gave voice to nearly the same reflections he had harbored earlier. He nearly missed her next remark.

"We would take the Aymará back to the old ways and past glory, purge the land of infidel foreigners and together people the earth with demigods and goddesses. Seven years have passed since then. You have grown to a man of twenty one years and I to a mature woman. The time has not yet come and still the outlanders remain. I am disturbed; life has quickened three times in my womb, only to be rejected by my body and cast out, unformed

and lifeless. Our faithful followers wonder. I
wonder. Why is this, my brother-husband?"

"The gods work in their own ways and
according to their own designs. When Veracocha chooses for you to bear live fruit, so shall
it be. Before then, though, we must restore the
old rites and purify our land. Come, let us
leave this place, meet with our followers and
lay a plan to capture our sacrifices."

12

FLEETING WINGS OF DEATH

"There is an intersecting tunnel ahead," the Penetrator told Sam and Mario when he returned from a short scouting trip. "According to my compass, the left branch leads toward the Akapana pyramid. The right runs only a short distance, then turns back in an L shape. Perhaps some sort of barracks arrangement."

"I'll check that out," Mario offered. "You two go on the other way. We'll meet back here."

"Okay. Make it in . . . say, fifteen minutes."

"That should do," Mario agreed with Mark.

Together they walked to the end of the tunnel and separated. The Penetrator counted paces until he came to the conclusion they had padded under the outer baseline of the pyramid. Now the featureless walls presented doorways and widened out farther along into an area of partitioned cubicles that could only be offices.

"Should I mention the obvious?" Mark whispered to Sam.

"Five will get you ten the builders of Tiahuanaco never set this up," she replied. "Oh, Mark, this is it. We've frround Krishna Mira."

"At least part of it."

He beckoned and she followed to a larger cubicle where the hum of electronic equipment could be heard beyond the partition. Voices came to them, speaking Russian in clipped sentences. The Penetrator strained his rusty memory of the language to make sense of them.

"There is no possibility of a malfunction, Comrade Doctor?"

"No, Comrade Yatsor," Dr. Moller replied. "Everything has checked out to plus-minus point zero-zero-one. We could run the test flight tomorrow if you wished."

"The rocket will not be ready. We need two more days for that. Then São Paulo will be visited by a typhus epidemic."

"Why not Yellow Rain, Comrade Major?"

"Use your head, Comrade Moller. That would forewarn the enemy of our capabilities and our intentions."

"You said yourself that within three to five days after the test, Krishna Mira would be activated. What could they do in that little time?"

"Perhaps too much. Remember, the American agents have yet to be captured or eliminated. They represent a danger we can ill afford to overlook. If they ever learn that the entire complex is located here in the ruins, a single bomb could destroy us."

Dr. Moller blanched and his agitation could be read in his voice. "The antenna is in an extremely vulnerable position at the top of the pyramid. As it is, it can only be exposed at night. But surely, the other side would never seriously consider bombing Tiahuanaco."

"You know the Americans. Do you think they would let a small collection of antiquities stand in the way of destroying a project with the importance of Krisha Mira?"

"You are right, comrade. I . . . I remember what they did to Dresden and Hamburg. And to Colón. That was wartime, of course. They might seek to be more discreet now."

"Which is why they have sent agents prowling around here. From now until the final launch of the missiles, nothing must happen to interrupt the countdown."

"I have done my part, Comrade Major. Agent Flash, Blue-X and Yellow Rain canisters have already left the depot for the launch sites. Chemical service officers and my technicians will be there to ensure safe installation of the payloads. If there is any failure, it will not be the fault of my department."

"I am overwhelmed with your confidence, Comrade Doctor," Yatsor replied dryly. "Your *Führer* managed to eliminate only a few paltry millions in his concentration camps. This will be an extermination the likes of which the world has never seen. In less than a week, when the horror dies down, the entire Western Hemisphere will be ours."

A stricken expression drained all the color from Sam's face when the Penetrator whispered a translation of this. Her pallor had a haunted quality about it, and her eyes seemed to be rear-projection screens upon which the death agonies of millions of innocent women and children were unreeled. Mark clamped a hand on her shoulder, forcing her out of her waking nightmare, and nodded in the direction from which they had come. They had learned what they came for. Now was the time for action, his stern face seemed to convey.

Back at the intersecting tunnel, Sam choked back a rising surge of revulsion. "Oh, my God, Mark. That man has to be insane."

"Anyone who follows Marxism is insane in my book. Yatsor is no worse than the men who assigned him here, or any other Russian for that matter. He probably has a family whom he loves, an old overstuffed chair, scuffed slippers and a favorite pipe, for all I know. He may like feeding goldfish or collecting postage stamps. But that doesn't detract from the fact that he is a vicious son of a bitch that I am going to take great personal pleasure in killing."

Astonished, Sam's mouth gaped and she reached out a hand toward him in sympathy. "I've never seen you like this before, Mark. You're always so cold, dispassionate about what you do."

The Penetrator shook his head in bitter consternation. He had seen too much, killed too often. "That's because this is the last time, Sam. I'm sick of it. Sometimes I feel like I waded hip-deep in a sea of blood. No more. Angie and I and the twins are going to take a long trip around the world. When we come back ... well, then we'll see. There are more windmills out there than I have lances to break tilting against them. Maybe I'm getting old. Maybe I'm just getting wise.

"But enough of this." He began opening his pack, from which he took blocks of C-4 plastic explosive. "There has to be some direct connection between this complex and the top platform of the pyramid. We're going to blow this place, seal it and then wait for the Reds to come swarming out the other way like ants in a hill full of water."

"No!" Mario exclaimed in a sharp whisper when he appeared around the intersecting tunnel wall. "We can't use explosives down here without checking with the deputy minister of culture. There's a lot of pressure to make sure nothing happens to the ruins."

"To hell with that," the Penetrator returned while he continued his work. "For all we know the archaeologists on this project might be working with the Russians. *Someone* has to know about all the digging going on down here."

For an instant, Mario looked shame-faced. "I think I know who it is. You were right about the backside of the tunnel network being a barracks," he went on before the Penetrator could make another comment. "There's a dormitory and sort of a dayroom. Some men and women were in there drinking coffee. Two wore uniforms of the ministry guard service and I recognized three more as employees."

"At least that helps explain how the Soviets found it so easy to set up inside the pyramid.

Another good reason for shutting down this operation right now."

"We need troops to handle this right," Mario protested. "There are too many of them. At least a hundred from the layout of the barracks. By the time I can get a counterguerrilla unit here, we can have clearance from the ministry."

"He's right, ah, Steve," Sam joined in. "Three against a hundred is not good odds."

"We have only two days before they testfire a rocket loaded with typhus." Mark's remark brought a pallor to Mario's face. "How long will it take to get troops here and obtain approval for the strike?"

"A day, two at most."

The Penetrator began gathering up his explosives. "I'll go along with you for that long. After that, I call the shots."

Mario seemed disinclined to press the issue and Sam bit at her lower lip and nodded. Together the three of them removed the explosive packages the Penetrator had placed at wall junctions and along the ceiling. When all had been returned to Mark's shoulder pack, he motioned for them to start along the tunnel.

"You two go ahead. I'll watch the back trail until you have the entrance open and the area round it secure."

The Penetrator went to the intersection and divided glances along the intersecting passage and back toward Sam and Mario until they disappeared up the short ladder. Then he began to back toward their exit.

Suddenly a tall, blond young man in a

technician's white laboratory smock rounded the corner. He jerked to a halt and stared unbelievingly at the apparition in black that confronted him.

"Kahk vee . . .?" he started to blurt out, intending to demand what the outlandish intruder was doing there.

The Penetrator didn't let him finish.

13

SINISTER REVELATION

The Penetrator took a quick pair of steps toward the Soviet technician and swung a solid *shuto* stroke to the base of his neck on the left side.

With a soft sigh, the Russian went to his knees. The Penetrator hit him again and the young man's eyes rolled up, exposing mostly white. Mark grabbed him by the collar and dragged him to the foot of the ladder.

"Give me a hand," he called upward, then began to boost his unconscious prisoner up the rungs toward the outside.

"What are we going to do with him?" Mario inquired when he and Mark stretched the technician out on the ground and shoved closed the hidden door.

"Take him along and interrogate him."

"Why? When he turns up missing, they will know we've discovered the way in."

"They'll know that when they discover the dead guard. What difference will it make?" the Penetrator asked rhetorically. "They can't dismantle this installation and set up somewhere else. There isn't time. And if they don't know where we are, they can never find us. We've regained the initiative and nothing Yatsor can do will change that. Let's get going."

Sam led the way. Behind her the Penetrator took their prisoner under the left armpit with one big hand, leaving the right free to wield his Sidewinder. Mario carried the unconscious Russian from the opposite side. Like darker shadows they ghosted from one Stygian pool to another.

"*Slooshigt'yeh!*" a voice called in Russian from a crumbled pile of stone.

The retreating trio froze and those commanded to listen heard nothing. After a long minute, the Penetrator motioned his companions onward.

They made twenty yards toward the edge of Kalasasaya plaza when a harsh command sounded behind.

"*Stoy!*"

"*Alto! Alto!*" another man yelled in Spanish.

"Keep moving," the Penetrator hissed.

A man-shaped silhouette blotted out the stars directly in front of Sam. She fired at him with the suppressed AMT .380 and missed. Instantly her left arm slashed down and across. A soft moan followed, which turned to a high-pitched, almost effeminate scream.

"*Ayiii! Socorro, socorro! Estoy cortando!*"

Sam stepped closer and brought an end to his cry for help with two .380 rounds in the forehead.

"It's C.Y.A. now, Mario," the Penetrator muttered.

"*Que?*"

"Cover your ass time."

"We had better leave him behind, then."

"No. I still want to get whatever I can out of him."

Three figures rushed toward the center of the disturbance. A machete blade glinted briefly in the starshine. The Penetrator squeezed off a three-round burst from the Sidewinder and one man pitched forward with a liquid, burbling grunt. One of the trio leaped at Mario.

The Bolivian army officer clubbed his assailant aside with a powerful swing of his arm, then fisted his Ballester-Molina and sent a suppressed .45 slug winging into his enemy's rib cage.

"*Pamagheet'yeh!*" the Penetrator shouted at the last one. "Help!" he repeated in Russian, freezing the burly man in place long enough for Sam to bury her Urban Skinner to her knuckles in his back.

The pointed tip, an inch of sharpened false edge and fine-honed cutting surface slid easily into flesh, piercing a kidney. The KGB bullyboy jolted forward in time to meet a four-finger spear hand thrust from the Penetrator.

Cartilage strained to the breaking point and crushed closed the Russian's throat. He sank, gagging, to the ground, numbed by the pain in his kidney and strangling on the blood that pooled in his trachea and seeped into his lungs. The Penetrator bent and hoisted the technician.

"Come on."

Footsteps pounded behind them, yet so far the enemy had failed to fire a single shot. Worried about defacing the antiquities, the Penetrator surmised, and giving themselves away. Ahead of him, Sam had reached the outer wall. Beyond, a healthy city-block run separated them from the fence.

A bullet cracked through the air and tugged at the sleeve of the Penetrator's jacket. Wrong, he decided. If they could keep it quiet, the Soviets were willing to take a risk. And why not? We're here, the Penetrator thought. That will force them into going all out to stop us from spreading the word. He stopped long enough to return fire.

An angry flash of red accompanied the insistent burr of the intercom. Irritated, Gregor Yatsor slapped at the key with a huge, hairy-backed hand. "Yes? What is it now?" he growled.

"The Americans have penetrated our security net, Comrade Major. A firefight has developed."

Yatsor slammed a big fist on his desk. "Impossible. The electronic alarms did not register."

"They are up here, all the same, Comrade Major."

"I'll send men to reinforce you." Yatsor cut the contact and depressed another switch. "Send a squad of men to the surface to engage the intruders," he snapped. "And have Lieutenant Galkin report to my office at once."

While he waited for the young KGB officer to appear, Gergor Yatsor puzzled over the failure of his extensive network of infrared, doppler and audio pickup devices. It seemed impossible that all three would malfunction at the same time. A knock sounded at the cubical door.

"Vigdeet'yeh!" he commanded.

Lt. Yuri Galkin entered as ordered. He alternately blinked his eyes and tried to rub sleep from them. "Lieutenant Galkin reporting as ordered, Comrade Major."

"You are going to lose a little sleep, Galkin," Yatsor announced after he returned the young lieutenant's salute. "The American agents have penetrated our defenses. How seriously I do not yet know. I want you to take five men, our people you understand, and go through the alternate tunnel to the motor pool. Take a car, something fast, and be ready to intercept the enemy if they manage to break clear of the compound. They must be stopped. I would prefer to be able to interrogate them, but if it appears they might get away, you are to kill them all. Leave at once."

"Yes, Comrade Major."

Galkin executed a snappy salute, fully awake now, pivoted sharply on one toe and marched from the room. He drew his sidearm and a SVD sniper rifle, equipped with the PSO-1 sight, that featured a four-power optical telescope, integral automatic rangefinder, battery-powered reticle illuminator and infrared mode for night use. Galkin knew exactly whom he wanted to handle that.

In the barracks wing, he located his man. "Corporal Semko, take this. We have a little job to do. Get Yakshov and Vakasov and two other men. We are leaving at once."

"Yes, Comrade Lieutenant. Who are we after?"

At this, Galkin paused. "I'm not certain. American agents are supposed to have entered the ruins up above. The Comrade Major wants us to be ready to cut them off if they try to escape outside the first fence."

In his office, Gregor Yatsor paced back and forth behind his desk, a limited space at best. "Damn all these Latins!" he exploded to Constantin Tyolpan, who had joined him. "Oquendo and Torreos have let us down miserably in this. It was their responsibility to provide an adequate security screen. To act as a buffer so that our activities went unremarked by the authorities. It hasn't worked that way. Like all Latins, they consider revolution a game, a traditional means of changing governments with no thought toward the future except to prepare for the next time. And these Bolivians are the worst of the lot.

"In the first one hundred twenty-seven years of her existence as a country, Bolivia had one hundred seventy-nine revolutions. That is more than one a year! They even have an old saying here that, 'Presidents do not know how to step down in time. They have to be shot out of office.' You see? With that type of attitude toward revolution, who is to say that the same men who help put our beloved Soviet Union in power here today won't be fighting against us in a year or two?"

"They are in Afghanistan," Tyolpan returned dryly.

Yatsor's face flushed a deep scarlet. "Don't mention that name! I will not tolerate it." Yatsor remained deeply conscious that the only blot on his otherwise exemplary record resulted from a catastrophic misevaluation of the sentiment of the Afghan people and their willingness to resist Soviet occupation. With an effort he regained his composure.

"I am sorry, Tulip. I should not have raged at you. It's these . . . these incompetents that Moscow has saddled me with. It affects my nerves. Now we have a sure chance of eliminating American interference once and for all. I've sent Lieutenant Galkin and five men to intercept the intruders, in the event they manage to evade our forces above."

"A good man. He should be more than able for the job."

"I thought so, too. I will be anxious to hear his report."

Two men stumbled, as though the earth had been kicked from under their feet. A pair of three-round bursts from the suppressed Sidewinder had accounted for the phenomenon. The Penetrator took time to peel his prisoner out of the white lab coat that made him a hazardous target in the night.

"There's the opening," Mario panted. "Only a little way to the fence."

"We'll have to carry this one," the Penetrator

gasped out. His lungs ached in the thin oxygen of the high-altitude plain. Small wisps of
blackness swam in his eyes from time to time
and he felt the tug of incipient nausea that
forewarned of *soroche*, high-altitude sickness.
With a feeling akin to misery, he remembered
the kilometer of ground they had to cover to
reach the Land Rover.

"Yes. Dragging him is too slow," Mario
agreed, concerned by that problem only, indif-
ferent to the fact that while they dragged the
unconscious Russian by his heels, the sharp-
edged rock of the compound cut into the bare
flesh of his back.

The Penetrator made another check of their
immediate area. He sought some sign of their
pursuer through the extension of his human
senses, made paranormal by the powers of
Sho-tu-ça, the warrior medicine of the Cheyenne
Dog Soldiers.

From the beginning of Mark's physical and
mental conditioning under David Red Eagle,
the aged medicine man taught him the secrets
of the Dog Soldier's uncanny prowess at night
stalking and pony raids against the traditional
enemies of the tribe. Unsurpassed by any other
society, the Dog Soldiers maintained an ability to see in darkness by a power that seemed
to duplicate that of infrared. On the blackest
of stormy nights, Mark discovered, he could
heighten the receptive ability of his retinas
and produce images, often slightly blurred, of
a yellow-green hue. Movement was easily dis-
cerned and even the presence and approximate type of a weapon intuited.

At first this strange new power disconcerted him. Red Eagle encouraged him and taught him more. After a while, in the game of survival against enormous odds, it became second nature. Mark appreciated his gift, and as his proficiency in the use of paranormal powers increased—in vision, hearing, heartbeat, breath control and the stopping of bleeding—Red Eagle introduced yet another superior talent.

Mark journeyed to Oklahoma, to the home of an aged Cherokee, known with honor by his people as Wind Walker. Red Eagle claimed that the old man had mastered the secret of how to move among people without being seen. At first Mark scoffed at it. Then he learned the hard way.

At the supper table one evening, Wind Walker simply ceased to be in his chair at the far end of the board. A moment later, Mark's stew bowl overturned. He blinked in surprised consternation and an instant later, Wind Walker reappeared in his proper place. It had taken the Penetrator many long months to master the technique. Once learned, it worked equally well as the powers of *Sho-tu-ča*. He had employed it against the Baja bandits of El Barón, in the small town of El Triunfo and again in his efforts to aid the people of the Taos Pueblo. Even now, while his eyes and ears scanned the distance for sign of the Russian enemy, he formulated a plan whereby he might take advantage once again of this occult science to assist in their escape.

"Over there," the Penetrator whispered to

Mario. The Bolivian army officer peered into
darkness and shook his head to indicate his
inability to make anything out of the irregular blob of tumbled stones the Penetrator had
pointed out. Mark eased his Sidewinder into
position.

"Get out a couple of those CN-DM grenades
and have them ready. When I fire, lob them
as fast as you can in the direction I shoot.
Then we make a try for the fence."

Mario rummaged in his shoulder pack and
produced the bulky canisters. "Ready."

The Penetrator squeezed through the pro-
gressive trigger to full auto and hosed down
the stone pile. A yelp of pain rewarded his
efforts. Beside him, Mario heaved first one
then the second gas grenade.

They went off with dull plops and a moment later men began to cough and cry out in
discomfort. The sound quickly changed to gagging and retching when the agent took hold.
The Penetrator's superior night vision let him
clearly see four figures break concealment and
stagger about, two bent double in the throes
of nausea. He coolly blasted them into the
arms of Karl Marx with the remaining rounds
in the magazine of the Sidewinder. He changed
for a fresh one and then he and Mario started
off with their burden.

Sam waited for them at the hole in the wire
to give covering fire if needed. Once outside,
the Penetrator called another halt. He took a
spherical M-34 fragmentation grenade from
his pack, straightened the safety-pin ends and
loosened it in its holes, then buried the small

bomb under a mound of rocks, leaving only the pull ring exposed. To this he attached a short length of wire. The other end he fastened to the cut-away flap of cyclone fence fabric. Whoever came through after them would receive a nasty surprise. Without a comment, he urged the others forward.

By the time they reached the Land Rover, half an hour later, the Penetrator had already called on the last of his reserves. Sam, he noticed, appeared even worse for her ordeal. Mario only breathed heavily and a light sheen of perspiration shone on his forehead.

"Martha, you drive. You'll have to use the lights if we want to make any time."

"What about him?" Sam managed between deep, shuddering gasps for breath.

"He comes along."

"Load him up then. I want to get away from here."

"No more than I," Mark returned.

He and Mario shoved the Russian technician who had had to be silenced once more on the way, into the rear of the Toyota four-wheeler and climbed aboard themselves. Mark thought back to the sound of the grenade blast, which had reached them only five minutes after their escape. He could visualize the bodies and assorted parts flying into the air, the ruins illuminated by a ghastly orange-red glow. Maybe, he speculated without conviction, it would end pursuit.

"Next stop, La Paz," Sam announced while the starter ground to life.

Two minutes after the Land Rover reached

the road and turned east, toward the distant
city of La Paz, a pair of headlights came into
view behind, closing fast.

"They're on to us," the Penetrator announced.
"Give it all you can, kid."

"This road is impossible!" Sam shouted
back. "The potholes nearly jerk the wheel out
of my hands."

"Hang on and go like hell."

Slowly the Russian vehicle closed with them.
The Penetrator removed the remaining three
grenades from his pack and laid them in his
lap. "Give me any grenades you have," he
instructed Mario.

The Bolivian soldier produced two more:
one of red smoke and the other a CN-DM
canister. Yellow-orange flame spurted from
the muzzle of the weapon in the hands of the
KGB trooper on the right-hand side of the
chase car. The Penetrator pulled the pin on
one of his fraggers, slipped the spoon and
counted a fast "one . . . two. . . ." He dropped
it out the tailgate.

Only thirty yards separated the two vehicles when the deadly object hit the center
ridge of the dirt road. It bounced once and
exploded close enough to shred the radiator
and turn the windshield into a wide network
of milky spiderwebs. The driver swerved and
slowed while his front-seat companion used
the butt of his AKM to smash out the suddenly opaqued glass. Then he accelerated, coming on hard.

The powerful KGB car sped toward them,
high beams clearly silhouetting the fleeing

trio. The Penetrator released another grenade, this time the gas, when the distance had narrowed to twenty yards.

A cloud of irritating vapor blossomed upward at the front bumper of the Zil and the Russian driver swerved violently in an attempt to escape the effects of the gas. Enough entered through the gaping hole where the windshield had been to make the three men inside gag and claw at their eyes for a short while before the racing night air whipped the fumes away. Once more the KGB wheelman floored the accelerator.

Bullets spanged off the metal of the Land Rover's body while the Zil bore down on the fleeing people inside. "That's about enough of that," the Penetrator declared.

He came to his knees and pulled the pin on an M-34. When the driver of the Zil brought his vehicle to within ten yards, the other two occupants firing wildly at the Land Rover, Mark pulled the pin and whipped his arm forward in a reasonable imitation of a Dan Fouts pass.

A loud clank announced the arrival of the hand grenade on the hood of the Zil. It bounced upward and added the forward motion of the car to its trajectory. It landed with a soft plop on the upholstery of the front seat. A second later, it went off.

The Zil appeared to expand like an overinflated balloon, swelling in all directions, illuminated from inside by the hell-fire brightness of the exploding grenade. Then bits and pieces, some human, most flaming, began to fly away from the luminescent hulk that, without conscious control, wavered from side to side for a few yards. Then the tires went and the shredded remains twice flipped trunk over hood, scattering blazing metal junk along the way. Behind the conflagration, the Penetrator saw another set of headlights, headed their way at bone-shattering speed.

"More company coming," he laconically announced. "Let's try for a little surprise." He peered ahead at the terrain illuminated by the Land Rover's headlights.

"There, Martha. Over that ridge. Stop this thing and broadside it. Kill the lights the moment we get over the crest."

"Right, Steve."

Three minutes passed, while the pursuing Soviets drew nearer, before the Land Rover crested a slight ridge and started down the opposite slope. Sam picked her spot, dowsed the lights and hit the brakes.

A tall column of dust grew around the slowing vehicle. It shuddered to a rocking halt and the Penetrator jumped from the open rear window. "Hand that pig farmer down to me," he told Mario. "Then everyone out. Bring the weapons and grenades."

The Penetrator and Mario carried the Russian technician off to one side, placing him behind a small outcrop of rock. Sam and Mario gathered close and the Penetrator issued instructions.

"Now we wait for the KGB to get here.

When they come over the rise, I pop the smoke. They may or may not avoid hitting the Land Rover. Either way, we all empty our weapons into their vehicle. Keep it up until there is no one alive. Then we wake Ivan here and have a little talk."

"Skar'yehyeh! Hurry up! Faster!" Lieutenant Yuri Galkin shouted over and over at his driver. Another three hundred meters and they would top that rise. At the rate they had been closing on the fleeing Americans, there wouldn't be much farther to go. Inwardly the young KGB lieutenant raged at the blasted ruin he had left behind that had once been Corporal Nikolai Semko and two trusted men. The Americans would not get the same chance with him, he vowed.

Then the Zil ground noisily into the incline, bumped violently over the ruts and at last topped the low crest. Instantly a curtain of red smoke billowed in front of them. Behind it, Lieutenant Galkin caught a wavering, indistinct glimpse of the Land Rover, broadsided in the road.

"Pasmatreet'yeh!" he shrieked at his driver, who had already begun to apply the brakes.

Yuri Galkin's warning to look out did no good, though. The car body began to resound like a giant drum to the continuous pounding of bullets. It rocked on its springs and glass disintegrated from the frames. Slugs bit into flesh and ripped apart uniform jackets. Blood squirted and splashed over the headliner and upholstery. Three bodies bounced and jigged to the tune of a full-auto death march.

Yuri Galkin had time for only one dispairing thought. "Mother!" he cried aloud. "Oh ... Mother!"

"All right, comrade, time to talk to us," the Penetrator said ten minutes later, after reviving the Soviet scientist and injecting him from the small kit of drugs he wore on his ankle. "What is your name?"

"B-Balnoy. Boris Balnoy. I am a Soviet citizen an' ... an' ... I ..."

"Never mind that, Boris. Answer my questions and everything will be all right. You are Boris Balnoy?"

"Y-yes. Boris Balnoy."

"You work on Krisha Mira?"

"Krish' ... v'ry secret. Krisha Mira ... top secret."

"That's all right, Boris," the Penetrator went on patiently. "We know all about Krisha Mira. We know about the transmitter," he suggested.

"Transmitter. Yes, big transmitter."

"And the antenna."

"Most complex antenna in the world," Balnoy told them, his inhibitions erased by a potent dosage of sodium pentothal.

"We know about the rockets, too."

"Rockets, to smash the imperialist West. Old fashion', though. Major Yatsor doesn't like them. Says they are unreliable. They are good. I checked them myself."

"Good for you, Boris. Now you see we do

know all about Krisha Mira. It is our duty to Mother Russia to know. Tell us about the payload. What payload will the rockets carry?" the Penetrator pressed on in soft-spoken, confidence-dripping Russian.

"All kinds."

"What do you mean?"

"All kinds. Chemical, biological. No nuclear, no explosive warheads. All laboratory things."

"Nerve gas?"

"Oh, yes. Sarin and Soman. They are obsolete, but we have big stocks. Might as well use them, eh? Sarin and Soman. Gay-Bay and Gay-Day agents. Kill quick."

"What else, Boris?"

Boris frowned a moment and licked dry lips. "Blue-X. An' . . . an' . . . I forgot."

"Think, Boris. This is important for the safety of the project. Think hard. What other material in the payloads?"

"Agent Pakaznoy. Yes. Lots of that. And Zholtenaya Dozh't. Yellow Rain," he repeated, "all over South America."

"The Flash and Yellow Rain," the Penetrator told his companions in an aside. "We were right on that. Boris, what are the targets? What places will the rockets go?"

"Do' know. Not all of them. All cities. Big cities. Rio, Buenas Aires, Caracas, Quito. Many, many cities."

"How many?"

"One hundred."

"When?"

"Three days. Five at the most. Then countries hit with rockets will be demanded to turn government over to loyal Marxist juntas. Whole West will surrender to the will of Mother Russia. *Meer Meeroo! Dah z'drafst'voo-yet Sohyooz Sov'yetskik Sohts'yaleestechesskik Respoblik!"*

The Penetrator's lips formed a grim line. What Balnoy told him verified what they had overheard in the underground complex. When Sam saw his dark scowl, she touched his arm lightly. "What did he say?"

Quickly Mark gave them a rundown. "He added that all the West would be forced to surrender to the will of Mother Russia. Then he shouted 'peace to the world'—Soviet *peace*, of course, meaning the enslavement of the rest of the world—and 'long live the Union of Soviet Socialist Republics.' " The Penetrator turned back to Balnoy. "Is there anything else you can tell us about Krisha Mira, Boris?"

Balnoy worked at it, his face mobile with his effort to concentrate. "No. Nothing. That is all I know. Do I pass the test, comrade?"

"Of course you do," the Penetrator told him. He stood and looked down at the Soviet technician. An expert in chemical weapons turned into a betrayer of his country by other chemicals. Ironic, the Penetrator thought. But fitting. From under his dark blue jacket, he brought out the High Standard .22 and placed the muzzle of the suppressor an inch from Boris Balnoy's left temple.

"Good-bye, Comrade Balnoy."

"Good-bye, comrade."

The Penetrator shot Balnoy twice in the head.

"Put him over there with those KGB types, Mario," the Penetrator instructed. "Then let's get on into La Paz. We all need a good night's sleep. Tomorrow get those troops enroute. We hit the complex tomorrow night. Then your people can clean out the launch sites. But . . . we must hurry. Hurry."

"Yatsor is going to destroy the Western Hemisphere if we fail."

14

SAM'S MISSING

In the pale white light of predawn, Gregor Yatsor stood beside the blackened rubble that had been a Zil sedan. Flames still flickered from one tire and tendrils of gray-black smoke rose in the chill, thin air, burnt-rubber-scented and ominous.

"Lieutenant Galkin?" he tersely inquired.

"Up ahead," A KGB man told him. "With Privates Vakasov and Mishkin and a technician named Balnoy. They are all dead. Shot."

"And the Americans?" Yatsor grunted. "Though I needn't ask. Any sign that even one of them was wounded?"

"None, Comrade Major."

Awe tinged Yatsor's next words. "What is it we are fighting here? One man, one woman and a Bolivian soldier. Impossible. No one can be that good . . . or that lucky," he added reluctantly. "We'll get them. Eventually they will make a mistake and we'll have them in our hands."

"There was a man like that . . ." the junior

138

agent began, then let it drop, not quite believing it himself.

"Who? What man? Speak up Ilya."

Ilya Korabin reluctantly formed his words. "Do you recall when Major Leizenka was disgraced and sent to Vladivostok?"

"Ah, yes. The Persis affair. I was on the Mideast control desk at the time."

"Rumor had it at the time, at least among us field agents, that the man responsible for freeing the American hostages and bringing censure down on Comrade Leizenka was a certain phenomenal American called the Penetrator."

Yatsor's lips tightened into a grim, disapproving line. "I heard that rumor, Comrade Korabin. Foolishness!" Yatsor's vehemence came largely from a sinking realization that his young subordinate might have come upon the answer to the seeming invincibility of these American agents. If the man was the Penetrator, even though the official opinion labeled him more myth than reality, that could account for it. He smothered his agitation with brusque orders.

"Arrange for the bodies to be taken care of. Make sure all of this debris is disposed of. We cannot risk the Bolivian authorities investigating. And send Oquendo and Torreos to me."

Half an hour later, safely back inside the complex by way of the hidden entrance outside the fifty-acre tract, Major Gregor Yatsor sat behind his desk, hands steepled together, and glowered at the Bolivian Communists.

They waited, steadily growing nervous at

the silence, eyes scanning the bare desk top, the single, four-drawer, metal file cabinet and spartan vista of unadorned walls. At last Yatsor cleared his throat. Torreos winced and Oquendo licked dry lips.

"It appears we fared little better than your people," the KGB major began. "You know of the situation last night? Now we must move on. So far we have been able to prevent the Americans from making a report to their control. When they die, what they know goes with them. Have you managed to get any line on their whereabouts?"

"Ah, yes, Comrade Yatsor," Oquendo began hesitantly. "At least on the woman. We believe she is staying at the Libertador or the Gloria. She has been seen at both hotels."

"Find her, then, and bring her here." When neither Bolivian made a move, Yatsor slammed his open palm on the desk. It resounded like a pistol shot. "That is all, comrades. Do as you are told."

After four hours of sound sleep, the Penetrator rapped lightly on the door to Sam's hotel room. He received no answer and knocked again. Still no response.

"Sam . . . it's me," he called softly, knuckles drumming on the upper panel a third time. Mark put his ear to the door and listened. He could not hear the shower running, so that was out. His hand touched the knob and tried it.

The latch clicked and the door swung open. Before him the room lay empty. "Sam!"

Quickly the Penetrator entered and closed the portal behind him. In swift strides he covered every corner of the room, the bath and closet. No sign of Sam. He did locate an overturned bedside table, the small terracotta lamp shattered on the floor. The bedclothes were in disarray. Mark spotted several small spatters of blood on the sheet, grisly Rorschach blots on a snowy bit of cloth. He reached for the telephone and dialed the number Mario Campos had given him.

"Mario," the Penetrator began when he had been switched through an endless chain of military pecking order. "Martha is missing."

"Where are you?"

"In her room. No sign of her and everything is in order except for a broken lamp and some blood spots."

"Maybe she went down for breakfast."

"No. I was to meet her here for that. Could the Soviets . . .?" he let it hang, unwilling to voice his suspicion.

"I'll be right there."

Captain Mario Campos left his office, his .45 auto carefully adjusted in the shoulder leather, and headed to the hotel. His mind worked over the difficulty he had encountered in getting orders cut for movement of the two counter-insurgent battalions from their regular posts to a point ten kilometers from Tiahuanaco.

Frustrated at every point by desk-bound field-grade officers with all the hidebound resistance of the worst sort of bureaucrat, he had at last had to go around channels. Mario had called the defense minister and the president. Cooperation came quickly then, although with dark hints that his career had been irreparably damaged by his insubordinate refusal to play the game by their rules, At least he had the satisfaction of knowing that the troops would be alerted and on the way by the time he reached the strange American, Steve Fletcher.

Thinking of Fletcher made him recall an intelligence brief that had routinely come across his desk a couple of years ago. It involved an American fully as cold and deadly as Esteban Fletcher. Believed to be a freelance assassin, not an employee of the Central Intelligence Agency or any other covert service, this man was known as the Penetrator. A strange name, Mario had thought at the time, yet no stranger than his alleged accomplishments.

This Penetrator was believed at that time to be responsible for the eradication of a large Nazi paramilitary force in neighboring Brazil. Good riddance to that kind, Mario thought again in his review of the case file. The incident had been close enough to home to cause the chief of intelligence to order a complete profile work-up on the man known as the Penetrator.

What had been uncovered, Mario considered nothing short of astonishing. The Penetrator was supposed to have conducted violent, not so covert operations in France, Canada, Mexico, Japan, North Korea, Panama, Guatemala and the Caribbean, not to mention more than twenty of the states in *los Estados Unidos*. A very busy boy by Mario's lights. And deadly. Untold hundreds, perhaps thousands, had died as a result of the Penetrator's actions. The Penetrator's profile exhibited every bit of the proficiency demonstrated by Steve Fletcher the previous night. Mario searched his memory file for a physical description of the Penetrator.

When he found it, an icy finger began to stir up the far corners of his brain.

In the lobby of the Libertador, Mario noticed two men who arrived after him. He recognized both as members of POR. If they had only now reached the hotel, he considered, they could have little to do with Martha's disappearance. He took the stairway and hurried up to her room.

The Penetrator sat sprawled in a chair, the telephone in his lap, while he tried to think through what-all had to be done. If Yatsor had Sam, everything came to a stop. The Russian would advance the date of the launch and the chemical and biological death of Krisha Mira would be spread over Central and South America before steps could be taken to stop it. He dialed the number given him by Pyotr Dvenynoy.

"Problems, Pyotr. Sam's disappeared. I'm in her room now without the slightest idea what the hell happened. Can you come over?"

"Right away. Any sign of a struggle?"

"Some. I think it might be . . . Yatsor."

"Hmmm. Not necessarily. His people could

have interrogated her there and terminated her. No need to take her elsewhere. Give me ten minutes, will you?"

"Right."

The Penetrator returned the handset to the cradle a moment before a knock sounded at the door. He rose and sat the instrument on the only upright table, then walked across the room.

"Come in, Mario."

"Two of Oquendo's top men in POR entered the hotel a little after me. If they had anything to do with Martha's disappearance, it would be unlikely they would come back."

"The Soviets could have handled it. They can move relatively unnoticed around the tourist hotels."

"Except for one thing. Martha would have made a disturbance of some sort. She's not the sort who would go with them without a struggle."

"So who, then? And why?" The Penetrator began to pace around the room, head bent in thought. If not the Russians, Sam's kidnapping seemed senseless. Although aware that other revolutionary and terrorist groups were active in Bolivia, Mark discounted the possibility that one of them had taken Sam to hold for ransom. In his nervous pacing, his toe struck a heavy metal object and he stooped to pick it up.

He had seen it before, he realized when he examined the flat copper disk. At the time he had given it no special significance. Some fake artifact Sam had purchased in a shop, he had assumed. Highly polished, semiprecious stones had been inlaid in the copper circle, in the form of an almost-human face, a stern, though motherly, visage. Worked around the figure were what could be called cabalistic symbols. Sam had little time for browsing through the shops since her arrival. Yet Mark knew her to be a compulsive collector. She would find something, even if only at the hotel curio shop. That's why he had not considered it of importance.

"What do you have there?" Mario asked, looking up from his own silent contemplation of the known facts.

"It looks like a reproduction of some Tiahuanaco artifact S—ah, Martha must have bought." Mark handed it to Mario.

Mario studied the piece with expert appraisal. He caressed it with fingers and thumb in deft, circular motions. Suddenly a glow fired his eyes. From one pocket he took a small penknife and extracted a blade.

"This isn't souvenir junk," he announced, prying at a nearly invisible crack that encompassed the ornamental face. "I'm willing to bet next year's salary on that."

A metallic scratching came from where he levered the knife blade. "There!" Mario exclaimed triumphantly. A thin copper dish, reminiscent of a soft plug in an automobile engine, fell away to reveal the rich, yellow-red glow of pure gold.

"This is the real thing, Steve. It's an article of incredible value, both in money and as a piece of history."

"But what is it?"

"It's the sun god, Viracocha, or the moon mother. I'm not sure which. It predates the Incas. Could she have picked it up at the ruins?"

"No. I'm sure she would have said something about it. Why would it have been encased in copper?"

"I don't know. Unless someone wanted it to be taken for a fake." Mario handled the three-inch diameter disk with the reverence reserved for old and precious objects.

"And Martha stumbled onto the plan to steal it? No," the Penetrator corrected himself. "That's going too far afield. We're not here to catch culture thieves. Who else would want its true nature to be concealed?"

"I'm working on that. No one I can think of . . . unless it was someone who used it for its original purpose."

"You mean . . . as an . . . object of worship?"

"Or a badge of rank for a priest or priestess. Or an amulet for protection from evil."

"In this day and age?" the Penetrator returned doubtfully.

"Why not? Most of the old Spanish laws against practicing of the native religions have been rescinded by the government since 1952. There are supposed to be several, ah, cults worshiping Viracocha or other ancient gods."

"That's heavy stuff you're laying out, Mario. Why would someone like that want to kidnap Martha?"

"Tonight is the dark of the moon. Traditionally a sacrifice was made to the moon mother for the safe return of her light. Before the rise of the Inca civilization, tradition has it that it was a *human* sacrifice. Also it is the time of the year when sacrifices were made to Viracocha to propitiate the god and bring back the light and warmth of the sun for another season. Sort of springtime rites. Those, also, were human sacrifices."

A cold shaft of premonition, a certainty of horrible dimensions, pierced the Penetrator's consciousness. Of a sudden he *knew*. Somehow, persons as yet unknown, had seized upon Sam as the ideal sacrifice in their primitive, blood-thirsty rituals.

"What do you know about these cults? Who runs them? Where are they located?"

A knock sounded that interrupted Mario's reply. Mark went to the door and opened it. "Come in, Pyotr. I think we're on to something. It's too unreal to believe, but I'm afraid it is the only answer we have that fits."

"Thank you, my friend. I am worried about Sam."

"Who is Sam?" Mario asked, instantly sure he knew.

"That's the name Pyotr knows Martha by. Oh, excuse me. Captain Mario Campos of Bolivian intelligence, this is Pyotr Dvenynoy. He's a Company man," the Penetrator added.

"So, I finally get to meet an out-in-the-open CIA operative?" Mario inquired while he rose and extended a hand for Pyotr to shake.

"Yes. My cover inside the Soviet operation has been blown. I suppose it will be a desk job for me from now on. Damn! How I hate the humidity around Langley in the summer and the cold and snow in winter."

The three men managed a brief chuckle. Then Mark briefly sketched in where their thinking had taken them. When he finished, Pyotr blinked and shook his head in uncertainty.

"Could this be true?"

"Only too true, I am afraid," Mario answered him. "I was about to fill Steve in on what I know of the cults. First off, there must be literally tens of thousands of persons who worship on an individual basis in the old ways. Not even Pedro de Vargas and the Inquisition could stamp that out. Second, there must be several thousand small groups, numbering from three to ten or so, who meet to celebrate the ancient rites related to pre-Inca beliefs. Thirdly, there are probably more than a dozen organized cults, though only three of them are of any size. Lastly, a number of pre-Inca rites and dances have been worked into otherwise Christian celebrations. In particular the *diablada*—the Devil Dance—and certain of the *wacas*, which represent planting or other agricultural rites. Some of these, the pre-Lenten carnival at La Paz and *la diablada* in Oruro, are due within the next two weeks or so. That's what has led me to suspect this might have a bearing on Martha's disappearance. It's either that or we are back to the Soviets, and as I said before, it looks like they are only now closing in."

A muffled exclamation came from the other side of the door, followed by hurriedly retreating footsteps. The Penetrator made the hall-way first, his suppressed High Standard in one hand.

Halfway to the stairs he saw two short, stocky Bolivians. In the next instant they spotted him and tried to draw weapons from under their coats. The Penetrator moved first.

His first slug ripped a trail of fire into the closer man's chest, collapsing his right lung. The POR gunman rose on tiptoes, like a startled ballerina, soft whistling sounds coming from his pinched, round mouth while he struggled to draw in vital oxygen. Thick, rich blood, with double the red-cell count of coastal dwellers, began to seep over his lips, slicking his chin with a wide, crimson smear.

Mark's second round gouged plaster from the wall where the second guerrilla had been standing, then moaned off down the way to bury itself in a casement farther along the hall. He didn't get a third shot when the POR man still living leaped a flight of stairs to the landing, convinced that a sprained ankle beat hell out of a bullet in the head.

"Drag that body back inside," the Penetrator ordered. Pyotr and Mario hurried to comply. Once more behind the security of the locked door, Mark turned to Mario.

"Out of the three larger cults, which one would you figure for something like this?" The arrival of Oquendo's POR gunmen had convinced Mark that no matter how outlandish, the theory Mario had advanced had to be right.

"One group is called the Sun and Moon

Society. It is the largest and the most militant in support of the old ways. It is led by a brother-and-sister team, who are incestuously married and who consider themselves the reincarnation of Huascar Capac and Yahuar Ocllo, the high priest and priestess of the sun and moon during the time when Tiahuanaco was a cultural and religious center, before the Inca conquest. So far, their activities have seemed harmless enough. They have started a movement to gather and catalog ancient music, translate dance songs from the Aymará language into Spanish, that sort of thing. And they have been active in the restoration of several old temple sites. Their interest in the religious rituals is believed to exceed antiquarian purposes. Because of that, they are kept under periodic surveillance. Recently, information was passed from the commandante of the central police barracks that they had dropped out of sight. To me, that makes them prime suspects in this kidnapping."

"Where would they hold such a ritual?" the Penetrator asked.

"Not on the land. It would be too easy for the police to learn of it and prevent it. My guess would be on one of the islands in Lake Titicaca. Most likely Sun Island or Moon Island. Sun Island is the larger of the two, a popular tourist stopover even though the temples are in ruin. A lot of work has been done on Moon Island. It is closed to tourists and restricted from visits by anyone except archaeologists. There are guards and watch dogs. The Temple of the Moon Mother is fully restored."

"Neither choice sounds good to me," the Penetrator replied after careful thought. "But we have to do something before Martha winds up feeding the fishes in Lake Titicaca."

"More likely as a feast for the faithful," Mario returned without any attempt at humor.

15

MOON MOTHER

When she awakened from a drug-induced stupor, Samantha Chase had no idea what had happened to her. A dull throb at the back of her head made her eyes pulse so that her vision seemed to undulate like a zoom lens gone wild: in-out, in-out. Slowly the room where she lay steadied and she could focus on her surroundings. Stone walls. Like those in a temple or a pyramid.

That would fit with her first impressions. Did the Soviets have her after all? Early in the morning—was it the same day?—two persons, a man and woman, burst into her hotel room. She had fought them, that much she recalled. Had, in fact, managed to cut the man with a vicious cross-body slash of her Urban Skinner. Strangely he had not made a sound, gave no indication he had been wounded. Grimly, silently, he went about his task of containing her so the woman could tie her up. Sam stabbed at him, using the recommended technique of a boxer's jab.

She had missed, Sam remembered ruefully,

striking instead the bedside table. Wood had splintered, and the shock of the blow traveled up her arm, though the comfortable, shock-absorbing handle had prevented injury to her hand and kept her from losing her grip. Only when the table tipped over, drawing her along, had things gone awry. Leopard quick, the men-acingly quiet man had pinned her arms to her sides and his accomplice had swiftly bound her ankles, then her hands. A dark, bitter-tasting liquid had been forced down her throat. And then . . . nothing. Until now.

Sam moved infinitesimally, tested her arms and legs. The bonds had been removed, she discovered. Slowly she turned her head. Although still daylight, an oil lamp, suspended by what appeared to be a gold chain, flickered in one corner. Definitely not the Russians' style. On a low table beneath it a deep bowl of fruit sat beside a large platter containing a still-smoking joint of roast lamb. Where in hell was she? Cautiously she sat up.

Her brain did arabesques inside her skull and she nearly slumped back into the comfort of the bedding mat, placed, she now saw, on a stone ledge that jutted from one wall. When the room steadied, a loud rumble from her stomach reminded her that she had not eaten in . . . how many hours? She rose and walked unsteadily to the table. She selected a mango, bit into it with white, even teeth and spat out a strip of peel, then munched the soft, flavorful pulp. The first burst of flavor caused her hunger to overcome cautiousness and she gulped down the fruit and immediately pared open an orange, sucking at its plentiful sweet juice. Next she lifted a bowl of thick *charqui* soup to her lips. The dried meat, probably llama meat she thought, potatoes, turnips and rice put substance into the empty places and she attacked the lamb more decorously. There were, she noted, no eating utensils. SOP for prisoners, her mind told her. Also, a sudden flash of intuition provided, for the Aymará Indians.

"You have returned from the other world," a voice spoke behind her in strangely accented Spanish.

Sam turned, blinking at the gold-and-feather-bedecked costume of the woman who faced her. "Where am I?"

"A natural question. You are at the Temple of the Moon Mother. It is on Moon Island."

"Who are you and why am I here?"

A slow smile spread on the woman's face. With a start, Sam realized that it had been she who attacked her at the hotel. "I am Yahuar Ocllo, sister-wife to Huascar Capac, and high priestess of the Moon Mother.

"That doesn't give me a lot," Sam said in English, then had to think through a reasonable translation in Spanish. Yahuar smiled at her . . . was it a smirk?

"When the time is proper, all will be revealed to you. We are here to celebrate the rebirth of the moon. Until you are called upon to fulfill your part in this solemn rite, relax, rest, eat all you wish. There is *chicha* to drink and water. Soon you will be bathed and dressed."

"What for?"

Again the enigmatic smile. A sudden presentiment gave Samantha Chase a vivid image of what might be in store. Clearly she saw the frescoes and miniature models she had admired and shivered over in Mexico City. Her inner eye once more took in the spectacle of the black-robed Aztec priests, blood-spattered, their obsidian knives dripping gore, who stood atop the Pyramid of the Sun, ripping the beating heart out of a living sacrifice. When the present returned to her, she found that Yahuar Ocllo had departed.

"Oh, no . . ." she moaned aloud. "Oh, please, God, no."

"We will have to wait until dark to approach the island," Mario told the Penetrator and Pyotr. "They could see a boat coming for miles otherwise."

"That puts off the attack on Kirsha Mira," the Penetrator observed. "But . . . damn, Martha comes first."

"You mean, Sam?" Mario asked dryly, glancing at Pyotr.

"Yeah," Mark sighed. "Sam. I'm more comfortable with that name anyway. Let's get on with it. We will want at least two boatloads of your counterinsurgency troops to go along. Will they be here in time?"

"Already on their way, diverted from the rendezvous point outside Tiahuanaco."

"Good. Now, weapons. Everything should be suppressed to provide maximum surprise effect. When we hit, we don't stop until we've

kicked ass and taken names all over the island.
I'll lead one section that will drive to wherever they have Sam. That's prime. Everything
else comes after. But we had better make a
clean sweep."

"You're a cold bastard, Steve," Mario observed. "Won't that be interfering with these
people's freedom to worship as they choose?"

"Carving Sam up like a Christmas turkey
just might interfere with *her* rights, don't you
think? What I want is to get Sam back alive
and in one piece. If these moon worshipers
are too busy trying to keep alive, they won't
have time to do anything to her. Dead or
alive, it's all the same to me, just so long as
they are neutralized."

Long, slanting rays of orange-red light came
from the setting sun when two attendants
came to take Sam for her bath. Already cere-
monial drums throbbed ceaselessly and the
high, nasal pitch of chanting came to her ears.
Despite her initial horror, Samantha had been
able to convince herself that she had, perhaps,
been mistaken. It allowed her to eat once
more. The two silent women, neither of whom
appeared to speak Spanish, directed her to a
large sunken marble basin, every bit like a
giant birdbath without a pedestal.

There they spoke to her at last, in the
Aymará language, making signs to indicate
she was to remove her clothes. When she
hesitated, their insistence became demonstra-
tive. With work-strong fingers they ripped her
blouse away and tugged at the split-skirted

bush outfit she wore. In bra and panties, she shivered in the chill air of sundown and a wave of misery swept over her, threatening to rob her of control. Hang in there, girl, she told herself. Long ago Mark would have known she was missing. He would be looking. And Mario, too. Somehow they would figure out what had happened and come to free her. She exercised indomitable will to convince herself of this. Gingerly she touched a toe to the water and recoiled at its tingling iciness.

"Go on, go on, Chosen One," the elder of her guards insisted in Aymará.

Grudgingly, without understanding the words, Sam complied. Instantly her flesh contracted into a moonscape of gooseflesh. The younger woman removed her clothing and entered the bath with Samantha. She used a delicately fired ceramic ladel to pour water over the pale-skinned woman, smiling all the while and muttering a chant under her breath. Next she took a large gold bowl from her companion and began to sprinkle a gray-brown substance over Sam's body.

A brackish tingle on the tip of Sam's tongue informed her that this adornment was raw, unrefined salt. Images from an old book she had once read, called *The Witches Grimorie*, came to her mind. In particular, she recalled a section entitled: "To Prepare for the Sabbath." Witches, too, used salt for purification. When the bath had been completed to her custodians' satisfaction, they motioned for her to get out.

Back in the room where she had been

confined, a richly ornamented robe of pure
white alpaca fleece was draped over her naked figure. She shuddered with relief at the
warmth. Then a gorgeous, hip-length mantle
of woven feathers was draped around her
shoulders, secured with a gold clasp. This
didn't seem all that bad after all, she told
herself. A tall headdress of nodding plumes
followed next. Her outfit was then completed
by a pair of opne-leather sandals, studded
with gold ornamental figures. About an hour
remained before moonrise, she estimated.
Bowing, her attendants left.

"Now what?" she asked aloud. No answer
came to her.

Most of her guessed-at hour had elapsed
when the stocky man whom she had cut with
her Urban Skinner appeared in the open
doorway. His gaudy costume completely concealed his wound. He made some sort of ritual gesture before entering and then stalked
around her, his lips moving, in some sort of
prayer she supposed. He held a long staff, its
surface covered with a bas relief of intertwined
serpents and a huge, benevolent sun figure
capping the top. In his other hand he had an
ornate feather fan. He stopped at last, directly in front of her, and spread wide both
arms.

"I am Huascar Capac, high priest of the
sun," he told her in Spanish. "Tonight I will
be serving only as an assistant. These rites
belong to the moon mother. Yahuar Ocllo will
preside over the prayers and sacrifice. On this
eve of our Moon Mother's rebirth, you are the

most fortunate of all women. Go forth to your meeting with her with a joyful heart, rejoicing that through you, the people will be led from darkness into light. In one hand you will carry a braided shock of *quinoa* and *canahui*, symbolic of the newly rising shoots that promise a bounty of life-giving grain for the people. In the other, the skin of a young llama, which represents the fruitfulness of our animals. Your spirit shall bear them to the Moon Mother to remind her of our needs and ensure her blessing."

"My . . . *spirit*?"

Capac scowled, indicating that this, or any other response, was not expected. "Call to her with a happy tongue. Beg of her for us, that all might live in peace and plenty. Say now that you are ready to rush to the arms of our blessed Moon Mother."

"I . . . a-am . . . ready." Samantha replied, though her voice and step faltered.

Outside the low stone hut, Samantha blinked in the wavering light of a dozen huge bonfires. Indistinct figures, stoic, frozen-faced, very Indian, lined the approach to the base of the truncated pyramid that formed the substructure of the Temple of the Moon Mother. They waved fronds of woven feathers and watched with curious, avid, obsidian eyes. A clutch of attendants surrounded Samantha and, at a signal from Capac, compelled her to walk forward. Swaying, uncertain of what awaited her though secretly convinced of the horrible consequences of climbing the pyramid, she relented to the pressure and shuffled ahead.

In front of the temple at the top, Yahuar Ocllo, garbed in a plated mantlet of exotic feathers, waited beside a large, oddly shaped altar. The long slab of stone, notched at its upper end, lay at an angle; deep grooves had been channeled into its upper surface near the sides, like those in an autopsy table. Samantha shuddered, her inner-self rebelling at going on, and mounted the first step.

All too soon she stood before the high priestess. Blazing torches and bonfires cast a stark reflection of the bizarre scene far out beyond the water's edge. Yahuar Ocllo made a gesture and the acolytes swiftly lifted Sam off her feet and stretched her out on the altar. The sudden realization of her worst expectations nearly unhinged her reason. She tried to struggle, but to no avail, while strong hands held her in place, her head in the notch, bent far back and downward so that her rib cage swelled upward, the skin taut. The front of her ornate costume was ripped open and Yahuar Ocllo approached, right arm lifted high, a glittering stone knife in her hand.

From a distance, where the men crouched expectantly on the low-riding *balsas*, the figures atop the temple platform looked tiny, like players in a puppet show. The watchers stirred nervously at the barbaric spectacle and several crossed themselves when the attendants placed Samantha on the altar.

"Give me that," the Penetrator snapped in a harsh whisper as he reached out to take a suppressed sniper rifle from the Bolivian soldier next to him in the bow of one boat. He took careful aim, caught a deep breath, released half of it and held the rest while his finger took the slack from the military trigger.

Only a muffled bark, like an apologetic, watery cough from a cold sufferer, sounded from the long suppressor tube on the M-95 rifle.

A fraction of a second later, Yahuar Ocllo's head exploded like a victim of the Scanners. Blood, fluids, brain tissue and bone chips splattered over her hovering cluster of acolytes and stained the white walls of the temple. The Moon Mother had her sacrifice, though not the one intended.

"Hit the beach!" the Penetrator whispered into his radio, conscious that they lay close enough to Tiahuanaco so that a gunshot could easily be heard by the enemy there. The boats leaped forward.

Bolivian soldiers poured from the vessels, silently flaming death spitting from their suppressed M-67 MEMS submachine guns. Members of the Sun and Moon Society died in the ranks they had formed for the ceremony, row after gory row that bathed the pebble-strewn ground with a flood of crimson. Mark, Mario and Pyotr separated from the rest and headed directly for the temple.

"Get to the top before someone does a job on Sam," the Penetrator ordered. Now, with his familiar Sidewinder, he blasted a swath through the throng of screaming, terrified cultists and bounded up the steps, two at a time. From behind him came an occasional bellow of anger from the troopers when they found the corpses of guards and dogs strewn among the as yet unreconstructed ruins. Each time the tempo of their killing increased. Halfway to the top, the Sidewinder's magazine ran dry. The Penetrator paused to replace it.

An ancient, flint-studded wooden blade rent the air close to his head. Flickering torchlight endowed it with an eerie semblance of life, a writhing, deadly serpent that struck at his body. Reflexively, the Penetrator jumped backward, his right arm swung up with the subgun that lay along his forearm, and then sharp pain traveled to his shoulder joint when the crude edge of the weapon bit into the alloy housing tube of the suppressor.

With the power of rage behind the blow, Huascar Capac managed to cleave nearly through the silencer. The Penetrator's ankle twisted on the edge of a step and he went to one knee, while he abandoned the Sidewinder and groped for another weapon.

Capac advanced, eyes glittering behind a gold face mask that depicted the sun god. His blade whispered through the air again and caused the Penetrator to retreat once more. Silently the dispassionate part of Mark's mind cried out to him. This has to be done in a way that will not attract attention. His right hand closed around the haft of his Bowie ax and drew it from the elk-hide scabbard fastened to his belt. It came free with a sussuration of metal on leather and the sharp edge glowed in the firelight. He turned another attack by Capac and sought to take the initiative.

His weight came down on the twisted ankle and the Penetrator winced while he swayed to one side, off balance. Instantly the ritual sword in Capac's hand sang through the air, so close as to disturb the dark hair atop Mark's head. Instead of retreating, the Penetrator leaped up a step, which put him on a level with his enemy.

"Defiler!" Capac shouted in his own language.

The softer wood of the sword peeled back in a deep notch when it met the keen, hard edge of the stainless-steel Bowie ax. The Penetrator took advantage of this momentary turn of events.

A savage twist of his powerful wrist nearly wrenched the long blade from Capac's grip. The enraged priest disengaged with considerable effort and took a step back. His lips worked in sinuous shapes while he mouthed a petition to ancient gods to aid him. Mark's ear caught a startling similarity in the words to a language he knew, one taught him by David Red Eagle.

"Hold!" The Penetrator shouted in the medicine language of *Huna*. "You do not have the forgiveness of my High Self, nor will you receive the guidance of the Spirit One whose aid you seek."

Incredulous, surprised beyond any ability to express himself, Huascar Capac took a stumbling step backward. This unspeakable filth of a foreigner had spoken to him in the sacred, secret language of the gods. How could that be?

In the same instant, the Penetrator's right hand snapped up and backward, cocked by his ear; then he released the Bowie ax in a full-turn throw.

The tip of the heavy throwing knife bit into flesh on the left side of Capac's chest and plunged inward to the haft. Sharp stainless steel bisected his heart and he hadn't time to cry out before he fell dead. His body convulsed once, mightily, then he lay still, the taut muscles slowly relaxing.

Mark retrieved his Bowie ax, wiped it clean on Capac's feather mantle, and ran the short distance up to the altar. With him came Mario and Pyotr.

Below them the battle slowly wound down, with only a handful of the cultists remaining alive to surrender. Sam rose from the stone that was to be her death bier and threw her arms around Mark, sobbing in relief at her reprieve.

Once he had calmed and soothed her, the Penetrator turned to his companions. "This has been done quietly enough. Now all we can hope for is that none of our Red-creep pals hear anything about it."

He surveyed the unearthly scene once more, then checked his watch. "Twelve-forty-five," he announced. "We'll attack Yatsor's Kirsha Mira tonight at twenty-two hundred hours."

16

RAISING THE ROOF

Passing the hours of the day, regardless of the endless stream of details to be worked out, orders to pass along and communications to coordinate, became most difficult for the Penetrator. The Cheyenne part of his being, conditioned by the years of teaching by David Red Eagle, demanded that he purify himself for the manner in which Huascar Capac had died. He had used Huna to take a human life. Because of this, his *Low Self*, unless purged in the sweat lodge, was irreparably flawed. So much so, as the teachings of Cheyenne medicine dictated, that he stood in jeopardy of losing his own life unless he performed the required rituals.

To do so, however, would be impossible at the time. Not enough time—at least two days—was available. Nor did he have the proper herbs, the lodge itself, or David Red Eagle to act as spirit guide. As a result, a persistent foreboding darkened his hours. In the early morning Samantha Chase had managed to send a coded message to Washington, describing all that had happened and outlining the possibility that the Russians had become aware of the presence of Bolivian troops through the rescue mission conducted the previous night. Mark had insisted on taking full responsibility for this deviation in plans and Sam had dutifully recorded it in her report.

As soon as the information had been dispatched, a curt reply came back, instructing them to wait for further orders from Washington. By three in the afternoon, nothing had been forthcoming. Mark and Sam, Mario and Pyotr sat in Mark's hotel room sipping at *pisco* sours and reviewing plans.

"You'll be leaving in half an hour to the troop assembly point?" the Penetrator asked Mario.

"Right. When you get word from Washington, how will you let me know?"

"If it's off, there's no sense in maintaining radio silence. If it's a go, you'll know in plenty time. Move within two kilometers of Tiahuanaco and stand by. You'll have no trouble telling when the demolition charges go off. When they do, move fast."

"What about prisoners?"

"What you do with the Bolivians is up to you. Any Russians or other Europeans who get past us, kill on sight."

"What if the government decides to only slap the Soviets' hands over this?" Pyotr inquired.

"Knowing what we do, I'm tempted to say 'to hell with it' and go on in. Kissing up to those bastards has lost a third of what was once the Free World. When this project is ready to be activated, all the negative publicity in the world wouldn't prevent them from using it. Our only hope to save the Western Hemisphere from Soviet domination is to strike before the test run. By their own timetable that gives us no more than thirty-six hours."

"Would you take that responsibility?" Mario inquired, a note of incredulity in his voice. "I mean, to defy your own government's policy, and that of the other affected nations, is a serious matter."

The Penetrator's eyes narrowed. "I'd walk into the Kremlin itself, and piss in Andropov's luncheon borsht if it would keep the Soviets from conquering the world without firing a shot."

The phone ran, interrupting any further comment.

"Bueno?" The Penetrator answered it, then listened for a moment and handed the receiver to Samantha. "For you, Sam."

"Yes?" Sam listened for the next thirty seconds while a tinny voice rattled in her ear. Her face paled, and she licked dry lips. "Do I have that right? Everything? Everyone? Yes . . . I will. And . . . thank you."

Numbly, Samantha handed the instrument back to the Penetrator. Her eyes held a distant look, like someone gazing on the fires of hell. "The strike is on. That was a man from state. He gave me the codeword for a complete sweep. Terminate everything at the Soviet project and all the workers, no prisoners, no mercy. W-when I asked back for verification, the president himself came on the line and repeated it. He wished us good luck.''

A collective sigh gusted from the three men facing her. ''That's it, then,'' the Penetrator said with forced heartiness. ''Time for you to go, Mario. We'll see you at the Akapana pyramid.''

After the Bolivian army officer left, the trio completed their preparations.

Eduardo Garza liked the early watch, eight until midnight. It gave a man enough time to sleep at night, during reasonable hours. His hand reached into the pouch at his waist and extracted two caco leaves. Methodically he worked them into his mouth, past large, buck teeth—a brown-skinned rabbit attacking a lettuce plant. The Sovieticos would have him flayed alive if they discovered he used the narcotic plant while on duty, he knew. All the same, he dismissed with a shrug, it didn't amount to anything. No harm done. And it did help pass the time. He stretched his arms and turned to gaze in another direction while his jaws worked, with bovine complacency, at the greenery between his teeth.

When the garrot dropped over his head at 22:05 hours, his fidgeting had disclosed his position.

Quickly the Penetrator snapped the thin bit of suspension line taut and gave it a twist, then pivoted and hoisted Eduardo off his feet, bent backward over his own strong back.

The stocky Bolivian struggled feebly, his narcotic-numbed brain only dimly recorded that he was in fact dying. When the frantic little motions ceased, the Penetrator lowered the corpse to the ground. He motioned Sam and Pyotr forward.

"The antenna has to be in the temple on top of the pyramid. We'll go there first. While I rig the charge, look for the entrance at that end."

Two more sentries waited at the base of the pyramid. Pyotor took the nearer, while the Penetrator slipped soundlessly through the shadows to the one by the far corner, away from the steps. Some sixth sense must have warned the man. He had started to turn toward the Penetrator, Soviet AKM at the ready, when starlight made a shimmering line of blue fire out of the edge of the Bowie ax.

Rigid steel smashed through flesh and bone. The heavy knife crashed down through the cortex of the brain and cleaved cleanly to the base of his skull. The unfortunate Bolivian Red went off to greet Lenin without a sound at his departure. The Penetrator eased the body to the ground and returned to where Sam and Pyotr waited.

"We can't be sure there aren't more guards at the top. Pyotr, use that night scope on your rifle. Sweep the place, then wait here a moment to cover us on the climb."

"Then I join you?"

"Right."

A third of the way up the steps, a slug from

the suppressed sniper rig snapped past the
Penetrator's left shoulder. It struck another
sentry at the base of his throat. He uttered a
nearly inaudible gurgle, pivoted and fell down
the stairway like a discarded sacrifice at an
Aztec religious festival. Mark made a circle of
thumb and forefinger and waved an okay at
Pyotr. Quickly he and Sam continued on.

Two more of the enemy appeared at the
low, narrow entrance to the small temple atop
the Akapana pyramid. Only thirty feet separated them from oncoming vengeance. Sam
sent a snap shot at one of them, which struck
the man in the fleshy part of his waist, an
inch above his hipbone. He cried out, more in
alarm than pain, and went to one knee.

Before he could take careful aim, two more
.380 slugs from the AMT Backup drilled into
his face. One slammed into the heavy resistance of a high, thick cheekbone, shattered it,
and hydrostatic shock popped out an eyeball,
to hang, swinging, from the distended optic
nerve, a grim tree ornament. The second went
in high in his full upper lip and angled upward to destroy a portion of his frontal lobe.
The dark, hooked slash of his nose, along with
the entrance wound, formed a macabre exclamation mark that graphically illustrated the
surprise he felt an instant before consciousness and life left him.

The Penetrator fired a single .45 round from
his suppressed Sidewinder that smashed the
receiver of a Type 56 Chicom assault rifle in
the hands of the dead man's companion.

Suddenly weaponless, the Bolivian rebel groped frantically at a machete that hung on the left side of his belt. He freed the blade a moment before another jacketed hollowpoint shattered his right humerus and carried bone chips from it into his abdomen. Following directly behind it, two more bullets sledge-hammered the taut muscles of his belly and turned his liver into mush. He sat down unexpectedly and, for a brief second, stared at the machete as though unaware of its function or how it got in his lap. A soulful moan flapped his slack lips, followed by a gout of dark, rich blood. Then he toppled onto his side.

"Inside, quick," the Penetrator directed Sam.

They entered and sprayed the area for good measure. No more opponents appeared to challenge them. Mark quickly found the crudely hacked archway that Pedro de Vargas had opened three centuries earlier. Cautiously he looked into the excavated area below the small stone structure.

"Looks clear," he announced after a tense second. Immediately he lowered himself through the gap and dropped lightly to the rough floor below.

"Should I stay up here in case of visitors?"

"Come on down, Sam. We'll be going into the complex from here. Where is Pyotr."

"Coming now, my friend," the CIA deep cover agent announced. "Catch my rifle."

Pyotr's sniper-scoped M-14 dropped through the opening, followed immediately by the burly Russian-American and Sam. Pyotr snapped on a bright battle lantern and swept the walls. The trio's eyes widened in surprise.

Tall metal tubes, like the bars of a jail cell, rose from the floor in three ranks, a cluster of at least fifty, the Penetrator estimated. They gleamed dully in the bright shaft from Pyotr's lamp.

"The antenna system," Sam whispered in awe.

"Right. Pyotr, start rigging cutting charges on the back line. Sam, take the middle and I'll do these. It doesn't matter where you put them, so long as these di-poles are made inoperative."

In half an hour, their task had been completed. Now the search for the hidden access began. On his second circuit of the room, the Penetrator found it. He signaled the others, and while Pyotr set the timer on the prima-cord-linked charges, he swung open the heavy stone block. Beyond it a red-lighted stope sloped downward.

"Here we go," he cautioned the others.

Resistance, when it came, was lighter than expected.

A trio of KGB types, in civilian trousers and slingshot undershirts, stepped into the corridor from a laboratory door, their AK-74 assault rifles at the ready. Bits and pieces of them, along with sudden, high-pressure sprays of blood, smeared the walls of the tunnel and they went down soundlessly without firing a shot. At the doorway into the chemical and biological lab, the Penetrator peeked inside and saw five men, each in his own manner reacting to the sudden appearance of doom.

Mark pulled the pin on an M-34 fragger while two of the white-coated technicians rushed toward idle weapons. He tossed it into the room and ran down the corridor with his companions. They reached a safe distance before the small bomb exploded with a shattering roar that pierced their earplugs. Slightly staggered by the confined ferocity, the Penetrator returned to check results.

Equipment had been smashed all over the lab and the occupants lay sprawled in grotesque postures of sudden death. Satisfied, he rejoined Sam and Pyotr and they advanced along the roughly hewn tunnel. Ahead lay the large cavern and its warren of cubical offices.

Here, people rushed about in frantic disorganization, spurred to action by the loud explosion of the grenade. In spite of his determination to carry out orders to the fullest, the Penetrator felt a growing revulsion to gunning down men armed with nothing more than broomsticks or a paperweight. Worse still were those who died in the murderous blasts of the Sidewinder with no means of defense at hand at all. Several, however, managed to reach the arms provided for their protection.

"Steve! Look out!" Pyotr shouted at the Penetrator when they rounded a corridor made of the flimsy panels of the office partitions.

Two KGB men, in military boots and trousers, naked from the waist up, burst upon them, Kalashnikov assault rifles blazing in their hands. Pyotr leaped for protection in an open cubicle. The Penetrator dived for the floor of the large cavern. He rolled to one side and fired a three-round burst at the nearer man.

Two slugs whipped past the Russian, but the third hit the ball joint of his femur, shattered his hip and dropped him painfully onto his knees. The Penetrator adjusted his aim and put a blood-seeping triangle into his abdomen, an inch to the left of his navel. Then Pyotr's pistol boomed and the other KGB goon did a partial backflip that ended when his shattered head crashed against the stone flooring.

"Let's get to that transmitter," the Penetrator yelled over the confusion. "We have to rig it before we can mop up."

"Where is it?"

"Over that way," Mark replied, pointing to the left.

Four men guarded the precious heart of Krisha Mira. Professionals, they laid down heavy fire that pinned the Penetrator and Pyotr Dvenynoy behind the insubstantial cover of office furniture in a cubicle halfway down the aisle from the transmitter.

Seven-point-six-two millimeter, steel-core bullets slammed into the metal side of a desk, moaning and whining inside as they bounced around the closed drawers in an attempt to get to the vulnerable flesh behind. Pyotr hugged the cold rock beneath them, while the Penetrator pulled another grenade from his battle harness and armed it.

The spherical object hurtled through the air and disappeared inside the transmitter room. A moment later the blast sounded. The Penetrator sprang up and charged, slamming out three-round bursts from his Sidewinder while he ran.

Inside, the grenade had done admirable damage. Only one of the defenders, badly wounded, remained alive. He feebly tried to raise his AK-47. The Penetrator shot him in the head. Then he used the remaining ammunition in the magazine to trash the transmitter console.

Pyotr joined him and, while the Penetrator changed magazines, removed the cover plate and placed a quarter-pound block of C-4 in among the printed circuit boards.

"How much time?"

The Penetrator checked his watch, calculating how many minutes had elapsed since the charge was armed on the antenna system. "Make it fifteen minutes. Then let's go hunting."

Doctor Siegfried Moller stepped from his private quarters into a world gone mad. Men and women rushed about, some armed, most racing toward the auxiliary tunnel that led to the motor pool, concealed beyond the perimeter fence at Tiahuanaco. The sound of a distant blast had roused him from a brief nap he took as routine after the evening meal. From closer now, another explosion reverberated in the underground complex, over near the transmitter. Ice swiftly encased his heart. He paused only a second before ducking back inside. He took a Suhl-made PM 9mm pistol from a drawer and worked the slide to chamber a round, then stepped back into the corridor.

"Achtung! Achtung!" he shouted at the sea of fear-blanked faces around him, his own anxiety robbing him of his command of Russian. The fools! Why didn't they listen to him? What was needed was order. In Hitler's Reich they had order and discipline. These stupid cattle would dash about, bumping into each other until whatever enemy had attacked them herded them together and finished them all off. But not he.

"Out of my way!" Dr. Moller bellowed in German. He pushed at the offending technicians and shouldered his way through to a clear space. He had to see about the transmitter, then attend to his laboratory. He hoped he would find them in good condition.

What he found, instead, was the Penetrator.

Mark Hardin looked up to see the heavy-set, gray-haired East German bearing down on him. In the same instant, Dr. Moller recognized an enemy and reached to his waist for the butt of the DDR copy of the Makarov pistol he carried. He managed to draw it before he felt an incredible pain in his chest, like a massive heart attack, only on the right-hand side. He saw a thin curl of smoke escape from the lips of the end wipe of the Sidewinder's suppressor, then glanced down at the trio of holes in his lab smock that slowly stained red.

He continued his draw, though, and fired a shot that gouged meat from the Penetrator's left shoulder half an inch below the arm socket. Then something odd happened to his vision. It seemed as though someone had turned out the bright overhead lights.

The Penetrator fired again, although Dr. Moller never felt the savage attack on his body by a trio of 185 grain JHP slugs that ripped apart his intestines and pulped his left kidney. His body, spewing blood, was flung backward against a partition and slid to a sitting position.

Memory cells in Siegfried Moller's brain flashed their last signals and he heard again the strains of the *"Horst Wessel."*

Mark stepped over the sprawled legs of the dying East German chemical warfare expert and headed along the corridor to an intersection with the main entrance tunnel. Pyotr had opted to take the direction in which many of the Russian technicians had run; Mark had no idea where Sam had gotten to.

"Sam!" he called out. "Where are you?"

"Down here," came a faint reply, punctuated by gunfire. "I'm holding the front door open."

Mark started that way, only to be knocked off his feet by a powerful body leaping on him from behind.

Constantin Tyolpan wrestled with the big man he had tackled around the middle. The Penetrator proved more of a handful than he had anticipated. An elbow, driven powerfully backward, forced the air from his lungs and his vision darkened a moment before an in-rushing draft of fresh oxygen revived him. Too late, though, for his opponent had broken free.

The Penetrator faced the wiry, muscular KGB agent in a low crouch. Their collision had knocked the Sidewinder from his grasp and it now lay behind the Soviet enforcer, who menaced him with big, iron-hard fists. Mark's hand went to the micarta handles of his Bowie ax, though he paused in midgrab. This one had a look of importance about him. Although not the bearlike Yatsor, he must be high up in the Soviet chain of command. Their bloody sweep through the underground complex had resulted in at least thirty deaths, but some of the Russian team had managed to escape. He had to know to where. Suddenly he wanted to take this Red butcher alive.

"You're not some cowardly technician," the Penetrator snapped at him in Russian. "What is your rank, Comrade KGB?"

Surprisingly, Tyolpan smiled. "You know that about me, eh? I am Captain Constantin Tyolpan of the State Security Police. There has been speculation that you do not work for our counterpart, the CIA. That you are the person known as the Penetrator?"

"That is correct."

"Then why do you fight us? We, after all, are working toward the same goals—to rid the Western World of corruption and decadence."

"And replace it with what? Slavery?"

Suddenly Tyolpan whipped a roundhouse kick, aimed for Mark's head.

It missed and the Penetrator countered with a *shuto* chop to the KGB agent's calf that left it numb and unresponsive. Quickly, while his opponent remained off balance, Mark moved in. A two-fisted flare punch to Tyolpan's exposed chest nearly stopped his heart. Tyolpan's face flushed crimson, then faded to a corpse-gray pallor. A *yon hon nukite* four-finger spear hand thrust to Tyolpan's solar plexus put the Soviet agent out of the battle. Mark recovered his Sidewinder and then dragged Tyolpan down the corridor by the collar to where Sam held off four determined KGB guards who still defended the dormitory wing.

The Penetrator moved their prisoner out of the line of fire and took out his last grenade. "Put a fresh magazine in that popgun of yours. When I give the word, empty it down the corridor while I make a run for the intersection. Then reload and cover me until the grenade goes off."

"Then what?"

"We leave this charnal house." Mark pulled the pin and tightly gripped the spoon. "Now."

Sam fired her Backup, keeping the slugs a safe distance from the Penetrator while he ran the short distance to the cross-tunnel. He slipped the spoon and made a quick two-count before hurling the grenade around into the startled faces of the four Russian soldiers.

Three seconds later the blast sent smoke and slivers of rock boiling down towards where Mark crouched beside Sam.

"Time to go."

"What about him?" Sam inquired with a nod toward Tyolpan.

"He comes with us. For a while, at least." He took a quick glance at his watch and forced himself into a trot. "Run!" he commanded. "We only have thirty seconds before the blasts."

17

"GREATER LOVE HATH . . ."

When the explosions came, the groundshock knocked Mark and Sam off their feet. A sheet of flame belched out the doorway of the Akapana pyramid temple followed by roiling clouds of dust and debris. Behind them, more fire and smoke shot up the shaft they had abandoned a scant three seconds before. Around them, all signs of resistance had ceased. In the distance, the Penetrator saw the headlights of approaching military vehicles. Mario and his counterinsurgence troops had started to move.

"Keep moving," he told Sam. "We're to pick up Pyotr over there somewhere. He found another exit tunnel and went along it. Leave the rest for the Bolivian army to handle."

Pyotr greeted them with a small wave and a resigned shrug. "The big fish all got away, I'm afraid."

"We know that. I'm counting on this one to tell us where." A glance at Tyolpan showed furtive movement on the KGB agent's part. The Penetrator struck with lightning speed, his powerful fingers forcing open the Russian's jaw, while those of his other hand probed inside Tyolpan's mouth. He withdrew a small ceramic phial. "No you don't. We want a few answers. Be nice and we may even let you defect."

Tylopan muttered in Russian the equivalent of, "In a pig's ass!" and glowered at them.

Mark produced his drug kit. "You know the game, Captain Tyolpan. It isn't played by those bleeding-heart rules about a prisoner's right to remain silent. Do you tell us voluntarily, or do I stick you?"

For a moment, Tylopan's throat moved convulsively and his lips writhed. Then he spoke with a rusty voice. "I, ah, am not overly fond of needles," he informed Mark in English. "What is it you wish to know?"

"Where has Gregor Yatsor gone?"

"Probably to the supply depot. He and several others left immediately the first grenade went off. They will want to round up our personnel and destroy the evidence, now that the project has been compromised."

"Where is this depot?"

"That is something I do not think I want to tell you."

The Penetrator shoved the hypodermic syringe close to Tyolpan's face. "Give that some more consideration."

Tyolpan cringed backward slightly and his eye darted away from the needle. "It is, ah, in the Beni department. On the Mojos Plain, near the Beni River. It is on a large *estancia*, with an airstrip. But you would not be permitted to land. The nearest place to go in would be Magdalena. From there you have to cut your way through the jungle and cross the tall grass plain.''

"What should we know about the place?"

Tyolpan thought a moment. "Nothing much. They have RPG rockets there for protection, and SA-7s and 8s for anti-aircraft defense. There is a reinforced platoon of troops on the *estancia*, along with some Bolivian comrades provided by Comrade Oquendo."

"Anything else?"

"No. Nothing."

"It's enough. Thank you," the Penetrator concluded. Then he injected Tyolpan with the liquid in the syringe. "That's curare," he told the Russian. "You'll be dead in less than thirty seconds."

Mario arranged transportation on an army C-47 of ancient vintage and dubious reliability. The pilot would pick up a cargo of farm produce at Magdalena, this being a common practice and the only way of moving fresh fruit and vegetables from the small farms of the Mojos Plain. The arrival of the Penetrator's party and the counterinsurgency troops would excite attention, though it was hoped not enough to have a message reach the *estancia* used by the Soviets before they could get into position to attack.

"Yatsor must not escape this time," the Penetrator told the expeditionary force in a briefing prior to takeoff. He described the barrel-chested, stocky Russian and Mario provided photographs of Ramón Oquendo.

"He is wanted by our government for treason and terrorist acts. Take him alive if you can, but he, too, must not get away," the young captain told his troops.

A few minutes later, Mark took his place in one of the fold-down bucket seats that lined the bulkheads of the cargo plane. Everything had been put aboard that would be needed. The twin radial engines coughed and spun their way to full-throated life and the antique bird taxied to the end of the runway. Two hours later, they landed at Magdalena.

"Now comes the hard part," Mario announced when the contingent had left town and the last road behind.

Ahead lay jungle, dense and interspersed with a wide variety of trees, like those of Southeast Asia. Beyond that came a vast, rolling prairie of tough, wiry grass similar to the Argentine's *pampas*, but at a high enough altitude to make the use of horses marginal at best. Roads did not exist, and without them neither did vehicles. From the description given by Tyolpan, the Penetrator and Mario worked out an estimated trip of twenty-five miles, a journey of a day and a half.

When the footpath they followed ended at a small collection of Chacobo Indian huts on the bank of a tributary stream, Mario commandeered enough *balsas* for the force to float along to the confluence of the Rio Beni. They reached the spot three hours before sunrise the next morning. Now only the grassland separated them from the target.

Mark consulted Mario, his face drawn and fatigue hanging heavily on him from the efforts of the past forty-eight hours. "How long now?"

"If the Russian told the truth, we should be there before noon. Otherwise there is a lot of ground to search around here. We would have to call in helicopters."

"That might scare them out," the Penetrator observed. "In any case, we'll do what's necessary."

At a quarter past twelve, they came upon three stone and wooden buildings at the approximate location indicated by Tyolpan. These housed not the enemy but peaceful farmers. In response to Mario's questions, one allowed that there was indeed a large *estancia* not far from there. He gave directions and the determined band set off.

The Penetrator, who walked with the point man, spotted the target first. The troops had been navigating a thick copse of trees and nearly stumbled out of the covering screen onto the end of a short, dirt runway. Half a mile away, at the far end of the strip, huddled a cluster of buildings, shimmering whitely in the afternoon sun. Through a pair of binoculars, the Penetrator observed feverish human activity.

"That's it," he breathed with satisfaction when he announced his news to Mario and his companions.

"Do we hit them now?" Sam asked.

"Everyone could use a rest first," the Penetrator decided aloud. "We'll take half an hour, have the troops eat a cold meal, Mario, and then you and I can work out a plan to spread them around the area so we can attack from all sides."

"That won't be easy in this open country. Maybe we should wait until dark, then attack at dawn."

"That could give Yatsor a chance to get away. Have them crawl through the grass if necessary. We can allow time for that. In fact, we can take until an hour before sundown."

Long, slanting rays from the lowering sun illuminated a lessening of activity on the *estancia*. A great deal of equipment remained to be crated up and a large pile of discards awaited burning. Yet in obedience to some signal unseen and unheard by the watchers in the tall grass, the workers laid aside their tools and burdens and walked toward two buildings. The dark-complected Bolivians went to the larger, the lighter-skinned Russians to the smaller.

"They are going to break for chow," the Penetrator whispered to Mario over a small handie-talkie. "Yatsor probably figures to have them work through the night and then leave early in the morning. I've counted three aircraft on the ground, being loaded, plus the five that flew in this afternoon. Make that your first target. Cripple or destroy all of them. Yatsor should be in that big ranch house seeing to the destruction of classified documents.

Sam, Pyotr and I will head directly there. Good luck, buddy."

"Hang loose, amigo."

Major Gregor Yatsor pushed away the plate before him. The steak had been only half consumed and the medley of potatoes, corn and squash barely nibbled at. The fare had been more than substantial, even more so than the borsht, boiled pork and potatoes of his childhood. And flavorful. Yet his present circumstances robbed him of appetite. How could he eat with any of his usual gusto with so much to do?

Documents. Baskets of them to be shredded and burned. Tons of equipment to be dismantled. The heavier to be destroyed in such a manner as to make them unrecognizable, the lighter to be loaded aboard aircraft and flown to safety. Men to be dispersed, with cover identities for his own people that would allow them to pass unnoticed through enemy countries and thus back to Russia. Worse to contemplate than all this was his own future.

Failure in so monumental a project would do irreparable damage to his career. Gone the promotion to colonel. Gone the favor of the premier and of his old friend Dmitri Ustinov. He would return to Moscow in disgrace. But return he must. It would be much better to fall in battle. That way, at least, his family would survive the blot on his record.

What of his family! The thought drove an ice dagger through his heart. What could little Gregor look forward to in the years to

come now that Krisha Mira lay in shambles
around his father' feet? Certainly not the patronage of Andropov and Ustinov. Scorn and
contempt from his schoolmates? Of that he
could be sure. Would his ostracism, in time,
drive him from the bosom of Mother Russia?
Would he grow bitter and come to hate the
Communist way rather than seek eagerly to
serve it? An anguish, greater than that engen-
dered by his own defeat, tore through the big
Russian bear. Abruptly he propelled himself
from the desk and yelled for an aide.

"Send Comrade Oquendo to me," Yatsor
ordered. Suddenly he felt a premonition that
the implacable pursuit of the American agents
had not ended. No word from Constantin could
mean he had been killed. Or worse still, captured and made to talk.

Concentrated fire from Mario's light-machine-
gun section ruptured the gas tanks of two
light cargo planes parked at the end of the
airstrip. Glowing tracer rounds flamed the
volatile aviation fuel, threatening all the other
craft nearby. Workmen shouted and ran, heed-
less of the bullets zinging around them, to
drag to safety their only means of escape.
More weapons opened up around the perimeter of the *estancia*.

Native Bolivians abandoned their allegiance
to Karl Marx and ran to escape the mael-
strom of deadly lead, leaving behind a handful of Soviets to face the charging soldiers of
the counterinsurgency force. In their midst
came the Penetrator, Samantha Chase and

Pyotr Dvenynoy. They headed directly toward the large, two-story stone structure of the main ranch house. Steel-core slugs from the defenders kicked up clots of turf near their feet. Short bursts from their own weapons minimized resistance until they reached a low wall.

"Sam, go around and cover the rear. Wait until you hear us open up, then lay down a heavy base of fire. We'll charge the building."

After Sam departed, Pyotr made a low-voiced observation. "They're not putting up much of a fight. None of them have even taken a shot at our backs."

"Don't tempt fate," the Penetrator returned. His thoughts turned inward, to his own gamble with the powers. A lot of blood lay on his spirit, not yet cleansed by purification. He felt thankful that this would soon be over. The image of Angie Dillon Hardin rose in his consciousness and he felt a surge of love and longing that nearly tore his heart. Then the smiling faces of Kevin and Karen floated in his inner eye, their naked bodies glistening from the waters of the black pool. Safe, all of them, in the Stronghold. Another pulse of affection coursed through him. Roughly he shoved these tender reflections aside. He could ill afford such emotions now; he would be with them before long.

"She should be there by now," Mark told Pyotr. "Let's hit it." The Sidewinder, its suppressor removed, roared loudly and the Penetrator rose.

A blast of AK fire came from one window on the ground floor, joined quickly by two more on the second story. The Penetrator pressed on in zigzag pattern, his goal the roofed-over front porch. To his right, Pyotr rushed a window and hurled a grenade inside.

After the crash of the hand bomb, an unnatural silence held over the *estancia* compound. "Steve!" Mario Campos called from a distance.

"Here," the Penetrator replied.

"We've suppressed all resistance outside. Only the house is left."

"Send some men for backup. Pyotr and I are going in now."

A dozen Bolivian soldiers double-timed to positions around the ranch headquarters and sighted their weapons. The Penetrator stepped back a foot and pointed the muzzle of his Sidewinder at the heavy, old-fashioned cast-iron door latch. He squeezed through to full auto and blasted it to shards of useless scrap.

Quickly he changed magazines and kicked open the tall hardwood panels. He entered in a long, low dive that ended in a shoulder roll. When he came upright, he looked into the firghtened face of Ramón Oquendo. In a panic, the Bolivian Communist fired his AK-74.

Steel-core slugs from the 5.56mm assault rifle scored the walls, blasted slivers from the floorboards and stitched the ceiling. Two tore long, ragged grooves of flesh from the Penetrator's back and another smashed into the small radio set clipped behind his left shoulder. Coolly, Mark raised the muzzle of his Sidewinder and pressed on the trigger.

Ramón Oquendo slammed backward into one wall, his mouth formed into an "oh!" of pain and surprise. A trio of .45-sized holes opened a slow flow of blood from his chest. Behind them, fragments of bone and lead had slashed his lungs, punctured his aorta and burst his heart. Tears formed and he blinked his eyes. Then his knees sagged and he slid down the wall, his ravaged back blown to shreds where the bullets had exited, painting a wide swath of slick, shiny red on the white-washed plaster. The Penetrator shot him again, in the head, for good measure.

The Penetrator rose to his feet, and a second later Pyotr burst in through the door. They started toward the staircase to the second floor when an amplified voice crackled out from above.

"Whoever is out there, listen to me! This is Major Gregor Yatsor of the KGB. I have in my hand a container that holds enough VR-55 nerve gas to kill every living thing within half a mile of this house. Withdraw at once or I shall release it. This is not what you Westerners call a, ah, bluff. I must be allowed to safely leave this place or we will all die together."

"Is he serious?" the Penetrator asked of Pyotr.

"I know him, through the project. And, yes, he means exactly what he says. He is ruined now, you know. It will go worse for him if he returns, alive, to Moscow. If he dies in battle, he will be a hero, even though Krisha Mira failed. Otherwise the blame will be entirely his."

"He surely has the antidote with him."

"Oh, no doubt. Though I seriously doubt he would use it. In my years out in the cold, even inside the USSR, I have seen or heard of several KGB officers committing suicide rather than face the recriminations over a botched project."

"There's only one way to handle it, then. We have to make him think we are going along."

"He might release the gas anyway. When they get this unstable, there's no predicting what a ranking KGB agent will do."

"We have to chance it." The Penetrator cupped his hands around his mouth and yelled up the stairwell. "Yatsor! Major Yatsor! This is Steve Fletcher, the American your men have been trying to stop."

"Ah, yes. My bourgeois capitalist nemesis. You have heard my terms. Act on them or suffer the consequences."

"We need a few minutes time. I must confer with the Bolivian troop commander and we have to start the men withdrawing. Give me five minutes."

A long silence followed. In his imagination, the Penetrator could hear the hissing of the gas as it escaped from the nozzle of the deadly cylinder.

"*Gospodin* Fletcher!" Gregor Yatsor's voice blared from the bullhorn. "I have decided to grant your request. Five minutes—exactly. But first, grant me one personal indulgence, eh? Are you the man known as the Penetrator?"

What the hell? Mark thought. In less than

an hour this man would be dead anyway. "Yes. I am he."

"Ah! I thought so. No one else could have accomplished so much with so little. I admire your dedication and courage. It is such a waste, though. You can never withstand the tide of the future. I shall escape from here and the Union of Soviet Socialist Republics will recoup from this disaster. Ultimately we shall overwhelm the decadent nations of the West."

"Save your rhetoric for your bosses in Moscow, Yatsor," the Penetrator snapped back. "The way I figure it, you'll need all the bullshit you have to get on their good side after this. I'm leaving the house now to talk with the others. You can start counting the time."

The Penetrator and Pyotr walked out the door and down the steps toward where Mario stood, with Sam at his side, his face blank with astonishment.

Gregor Yatsor breathed a heavy sigh of relief and set aside the hand-held loudspeaker. He had doubted that the American would agree to his demand. Carefully he had prepared himself to die, leaving a note for his wife and children, a final report to his superiors. Now his earlier fears and the truth of what this American, Fletcher, told him began to weigh on his nerves. What to do? Could he trust them to keep to the agreement? With a shaking hand, he poured himself a large glass of vodka and sardonically toasted the glory of the Soviet Union.

*   *   *

"It's our only chance, the Penetrator argued. "Take Sam with you, Mario. Withdraw all the troops to at least a mile from here. Then Pyotr and I will go in after Yatsor."

"The risk is too great."

"No, it's not. Form the men up in ranks. We'll all start out together. There will be too many for Yatsor to notice when Pyotr and I drop out. Besides, the wounded will create some confusion, with people running back and forth to tend to them. Can you give me an alternative?"

"Wait and have his plane shot out of the sky."

"And what if he takes along the VR-55? Where will it land? If it hits the ground from any height, you can be sure it will go off."

Mario pulled a long, sorrowful face. "You are asking for it, my friend."

"That's why I want everyone at least a mile away before we make a move. Reduce the risk to the lowest possible number."

Mario sighed. "All right. If . . . if you can see no other way. I admit I can't."

"Good. Form the men up in front of the house where Yatsor can see. And, Sam, stay right beside Mario."

"No. I'm staying, too."

"Not as long as I am upright. Do as you are told for once. And . . . Sam . . . I . . . At one time it could have been you."

"I know. I'd like to meet her sometime."

"I'll introduce you when we get back to the States."

"That's a deal. Stay tough, guy."

"You, too." The Penetrator squared his shoulders and moved away from her.

"Yatsor!" The voice came from outside the house.

Gregor Yatsor roused himself from his dark thoughts and crossed to the window, the cylinder of nerve gas under one arm, the bullhorn in his other hand. To his discomfort he noticed that his body trembled slightly.

"I am here," he announced.

"We are leaving now. We will march out in formation so you can see that we do give you a chance to make good your escape. It will take half an hour to get far enough to be no threat. By that time, you can take an airplane and leave."

Yatsor allowed himself a humorless smile. The American had won everything after all. To what would he be returning? Even so, to deprive them of the ultimate victory in capturing him would be some compensation. Perhaps it might even work in his favor at the review board.

"Very well. I will keep my word and not release the gas."

Yatsor watched while the long file of men marched away from the *estancia*. When they dwindled in size to a point where they were indistinguishable from grazing animals in the distance, he turned away from the window, satisfied at last. He waited through fifteen more minutes, while tension made fiery hooks of his nerve ends. Then he gathered a few items, tucked the nerve-gas canister securely under his left arm and started downstairs. He reached the hallway and started toward the main entrance when a brief flicker of movement attracted his attention to a side room.

He turned that way and came face-to-face with the Penetrator.

With amazing speed, Gregor Yatsor forced his right hand to release the small grip he carried and flash to the arming mechanism of the gas cylinder. He yanked free the safety wire and released the valve.

A colorless, tasteless, odorless spray of the thickened Soman—VR-55—gushed out into the hall and room in front of the KGB major. It expanded rapidly, filling the entire lower floor area. In the last instant, self-preservation overcame the Russian and he reached for the needle-tipped tube of antidote.

Before he could inject it, the Penetrator's Sidewinder roared and Yatsor's head exploded into a thousand bits of bone, brain tissue and globules of bright crimson blood. A reflex action squirted the counteractive drug out in a yellow stream that splattered one wall.

On the floor at his feet, the cylinder continued to hiss expelling its deadly vapors.

18

REQUIEM

Peals of laughter echoed off the cavernous walls of the bottom level of the Stronghold. It would make the task no easier, David Red Eagle thought as he proceeded toward the black pool. Bright spotlights illuminated the heaving ebony surface, accentuating the two white-blond heads that bobbed near the middle and striking glittering shards of dazzle from the waves. On the bank lay two pairs of moccasins, abandoned along with a loincloth and a fringed, buckskin dress.

"Kevin . . . Karen!" the old Indian called, his voice more weary and careworn than ever before. "Come in, please."

The twins paddled to the shore and lay, floating full length on their bellies. "What is it?" Kevin inquired. Then he brightened. "Dad! It's Dad. He's come back!"

Scalding tears formed suddenly and flowed silently down the wrinkled, leathery cheeks, and Red Eagle's shoulders bowed under the tremendous burden of the sorrowful message he had to deliver.

"No, Kevin. He has not come home—yet. He will never come again. He now rides with the Spirits, in that place beyond."

Shock drove the smiling, joyful expression from Kevin's face. He and his sister went deathly pale under their bronze tans and both began to sob uncontrollably.

"Dead? No! Mark can't be dead!" Kevin howled in a consuming agony of grief. *"He can't be!"*

"It is true. I know how you loved him ... and how he loved you. My own sorrow is great enough to burst this old heart. If I could deny it, I would. Even so, he now rests on the plains of endless grass and abundant buffalo. Gone past even the reach of our tears."

Unmindful, as always, of their nakedness, the children rushed from the water and clung tightly to the ancient medicine chief, wetting his buckskin leggings with their bitter tears and shaking his spare frame with the violence of their agony. Suddenly a catch in Kevin's throat arrested his lamentations.

"Mom? Does she ... does she know?"

"Yes. I have told her. You must go now and comfort her."

Quickly the twins dressed and hurried away, Karen's voice keening with heartbreak. Behind them, Red Eagle looked about this room that had known so much of the sweet taste of victory, and recently the joyful bonds of family love.

Never again, he thought to himself, shall these old eyes gaze upon this place. My usefulness is finished. The greatest warrior the Chey-

enne nation has ever spawned is dead. And
. . . *it is because somehow I failed!*

Following a solemn requiem Mass at the
church in Barstow, from which Angie, Kevin
and Karen were led, inconsolate in their grief,
a coffin was placed to rest in the nearby
cemetery. Then the principal mourners, accompanied by Dan Griggs, Kelly Patterson
and Samantha Chase, returned to the Stronghold.

There, the real funeral of Mark Hardin was
held.

High on an isolated plateau, far from the
sometimes eyes of prospectors, desert buffs
and nosy health department officers, a scaf-
fold in the traditional form of Cheyenne buri-
als had been erected by Red Eagle and Kevin
Hardin, who had taken that name with a fiery pride that shined through even his blackest remorse. There Mark's body, wrapped in a
buffalo robe, a bow, quiver and lance at his
sides, a bull-hide shield hanging to one corner,
was at last laid to rest. The empty coffin would
rest unnoticed in the graveyard.

Here, though, with his face exposed to the
elements, the Penetrator would find his last-
ing peace. And his spirit, unhampered by the
dark, dank earth, would fly freely to the land
of the shades, to hunt and ride with his brothers of the Dog Soldier society.

When all had gathered, Red Eagle led forward a young Appaloosa stallion and tied his
rawhide hackamore to one upright pole. Now
all tears had dried and a sensation of sub-

dued excitement seemed to ripple through the mourners. At a nod from Red Eagle, Kevin took up the drum and began a slow beat.

His sweet soprano voice blended with that of his sister in the Cheyenne death song. Red Eagle raised his voice in praise of the virtues of the deceased and harangued the Great Spirit to take notice of the rising spirit. Then he took a flint knife from his waistline and cut the pony's throat.

When it had went to its knees, sent along to provide a suitable mount for the hunt, all turned away.

"He was one hell of a guy," Captain Kelly Patterson of the Los Angeles Sheriff's Department said thickly, fighting the lump in his throat.

"There's never been one like him," Dan Griggs responded. He brushed at unbidden moisture that formed in his eyes.

"Oh, God, how awful," Samantha Chase sobbed, unable to control her sorrow. "T-there'll never be another like him, either."

The unhappy group passed beyond hearing and sight of the funeral bier. Even Red Eagle, his sorrowful duty done, turned to walk sadly away.

"Oh, yes there will!" Kevin Hardin spoke tightly. His face had gone white with the effort of controlling his emotions and his hand shook when he sat the drum aside. "I swear by the Great Spirit that I will avenge him on all those who sought his death! *I swear it!*"